IN VIRGIL'S FOOTSTEPS

BOOK II OF THE INSPECTOR QUEBERON MYSTERIES

JOANNA PATERSON

Copyright © 2020 by JOANNA PATERSON

All rights reserved.

No part of this book may be reproduced in any form or by any electronic or mechanical means, including information storage and retrieval systems, without written permission from the author, except for the use of brief quotations in a book review.

Illustration by Joanna Paterson.

Published by Sibyl Press. *It seemed to her she was making friends at last—ones that carried the wisdom of the past into the present.*

www.sibylpress.com

ALSO BY JOANNA PATERSON

The Smile of the Sibyl: Book I of the Inspector Queberon Mysteries

Through the Mirror Tales and Stories

The Shaman Birches of Argyll

The Wind Whispering

The Travelling Moon

Celestial Lights

CONTENTS

UP IN THE AIR	1
DOWN TO EARTH	8
BREAKFAST	12
HOLIDAY PLANS	21
THE RIVER GOD THAMES	29
RAILWAY JOURNEY	36
IN BATH	45
ABDULLAH	54
IN THE SPREAD EAGLE	62
ON GOING TO BED	71
IN THE INSPECTOR'S MIND	76
IN ELIZABETH'S EYES	88
THE TEMPLE OF APOLLO	97
TOGETHER, YET APART	107
THE PANTHEON	119
IN THE HANGING WOOD	127
IN HONOUR OF ALFRED'S TOWER	134
LOST BUT FOUND	144
ESCAPE	150
EYE-CATCHING	157
LOVE IS IN THE EYE OF THE BEHOLDER	168
STOURHEAD REVISITED	176

A Note From Author Joanna Paterson   185
Acknowledgments   187

UP IN THE AIR

Elizabeth was high above the earth. The clouds roiled uncharted and London was somewhere ahead and Scotland receding behind, a dot on the map.

She looked out of the window, anxious to be back on firm ground.

Her eyes encountered an estuary. She saw tree forms etched in the sand. Their branches showed a tantalizing, flickering brightness. The sand was wet and shifting; the trees moving as if alive. She became attached to their shape and sparkling reality. They entered her feelings. Although floating and transient, their passing presence nonetheless knitted firmly into her soul.

She was momentarily rid of the fragmentary. Creativity set in sand, fluctuating and shifting, gave her a sense of adventure. The picture was ephemeral. But she would carry with her the moving liveliness of tree forms.

She thought that even if her work would be like a book lost on a library shelf and she herself forgotten, Nature would endure.

It takes love to see trees in the sand, she knew.

Elizabeth watched as the landscape below was replaced by the grey and white swirl of clouds. A cold stream of air conditioning was wafting toward her. She was en route to the Stourhead landscape garden. First London, then Bath, then Stourhead.

Lost though she was in contemplation, gradually the face of a charming old lady attracted her attention, occupying the seat beside her. The old lady became very visible. She flexed her knees, crossing her legs in expensive cashmere trousers and a lightweight woven jumper knitted in an old-fashioned pattern. She was dressed warmly, armed against the cold circulation of air, but appeared very much in command.

"Where are you going on your journey, if I may ask?" the charming old lady said. "Your hands are unconsciously fidgeting. You must be deep in thought. I'm really interested, for your quest intrigues me."

She pulled a tight scarf of scrolled white lace more tightly around her neck. She went on speaking, her face rosy but pale, flickering with smiles.

"So sorry to deflect your thoughts, but I'm practicing being a mind-reader. I feel drawn to you as I can outwardly read your face, and inwardly I am aware of a determined, but lonely lady."

Her smiles broke up in crinkles. "You are thinking to stop in London, but to go on to Stourhead. What a lovely idea—but you'll be kind enough to think of me there. You'll need to," and she laughed, "because in even those enchanted woods and temples, there is good and evil."

Elizabeth stared back into those endless, starry eyes. In a way she was cowed, although she'd never admit it.

"I'm set on investigating designed landscape. I'm going to London. But I'm focussing on Stourhead. You guessed rightly. And since you are wanting to know out loud what I mean to do—here it is.

"Stourhead still exists as one of the few landscape gardens where the gods and goddesses and the river source give me much to think about and explore. It is designed in pictures and they have meanings. I want to explore and emphasize these meanings in designed landscapes and what should linger in us as we look at them. What it is that should focus our minds."

Silently Elizabeth thought, if I keep at her with complicated thoughts, she'll quit. She'll ask for some invigorating coffee.

"I'll examine first one of the great river gods in London, the River God Thames. He may reside in loneliness in Somerset House, but he'll reveal much about flowing waters."

The charming old lady shifted closer, exuding an ethereal scent. Her bright eyes, brown, in an angular face, were still fixed on Elizabeth. Her iron-grey hair was caught in a bun with diamond clips. Her eyes—and the diamonds—drew the light.

Elizabeth sighed and offered up more answers; what she knew up to now.

"The valley of Stourhead marks the well-springs of the Stour River, an ever flowing tribute to eternally vivid, eternally active, tumbling water. Henry Hoare the Magnificent, who envisioned and built Stourhead, touched the Otherworld in his Pantheon and in his grotto, revering the River God Stour."

She reflected on what she knew, and then volunteered what was so often in her mind.

"I can't help thinking, others will see too that water and earth are linked like children of the same parents, and are like the stars that seem so distant. Yet, for centuries, they have revolved night and day over our heads. We just have to look.

"None of the gods are lame gods, nor are they only works of art," she concluded.

The charming old lady seemed to weigh up Elizabeth's seriousness.

"All right," said Elizabeth, "I am adamant that people must deeply internalise more than just acknowledging what is before them. I know this is complicated. But I want to strengthen the idea that a picture, especially a thought-out landscape, means looking and realizing what is before you. This will then affect how you feel, how your spirit reacts.

"That which appears mute isn't. Even seeing a single moving tree means it has a message, is whispering to you: you sense it is there for a purpose. You become more acutely aware."

She was sharing too much, she thought. It was, after all, her own search for meaning.

"This should bring a welling up of relationship, of how you are related, how images are not just impersonal objects." And Elizabeth sighed deeply. She felt she was isolating herself and would be, ever so politely, left to brood.

The sparkling old lady glittered with her light-catching diamonds and seemed to transcend any complication. Stourhead mattered to her and she smiled at Elizabeth's mission and entanglement.

They rumbled quietly in accord as the airplane sped onward—a metal, winged seabird glinting in the sky. The lockers overhead leaned forward, seeming to watch, silently attentive. Travel was no ordinary feat and the manufactured air of the cabin a circling of sighs and groans, never abating. Airborne spaces were eerie, alive and apprehensive, always watchful.

The voice of the charming old lady tarried softly in Elizabeth's hearing. "My name is Mrs. Grimm but call me Gretel. I've been meaning to find you in Stourhead, but I saw you here and I have run into you by my own good fortune. And because I told myself I must. I've come a long way and you mustn't mind this intrusion, this ... intervention of mine ..."

Gretel Grimm composed herself, glittered more profoundly.

"My pleasure is the countryside and its wisdom in stories told over and over and yet so often seen as fanciful. People encounter actions but don't see consequences. Landscapes and stories are longer lasting than you think. Places have an effect on you ... and therefore they call out my presence. I *am* the hidden presence."

The vision smiled again and in an instant the clouds disappeared. The vistas below turned to wink at Elizabeth and closeness was replaced by an unending empty, sunlit landscape.

"Stories," said Gretel Grimm, "are my trademark."

. . .

IT MUST HAVE BEEN AN ILLUSION. Elizabeth distracted herself and concentrated on the clouds which were there again in their whispery and pale white. They enveloped the airplane, and they assembled higher, ever higher, in random collections, like wayward thoughts or flocks of woolly sheep.

Slowly the land far below emerged, touching her consciousness as forever there and not there. The clouds parted. Where oceans met saltmarsh and pasture, there just beyond the edge, were the sands, always moving, painting the landscape, heaping, then curved in wonderful writhing passages.

Perhaps, Elizabeth thought suddenly, Mrs. Grimm's suggestion was like a finger pointing towards Stourhead and the emotions evoked there. That should be where she, Elizabeth, should focus? Where spiritual and earthly meanings should be combined?

DOWN TO EARTH

Elizabeth walked alone to the conveyer belt and carted her luggage downstairs to the railway lines. She hauled her suitcase and heaved it up as the train took her to Victoria Station. From there she would hail a taxi and find a room in her London hotel.

Elizabeth attended to all the shoving and gathering needed. Down to earth was not a state of puzzled wonder, a state of testing the mind, of meditation. It was there to get the mundane done.

The woman at reception asked the usual questions and signed her in. She had an upper-floor room to herself that was habitable, away from the noise of the city. Her room was as far away as anyone could get.

High on the sixth floor, she could just see below.

The taillights and headlights of cars grumbled and screeched past.

She hoped, never-the-less, that she would be comfortable between pristine sheets and what appeared to be a snuggly duvet.

From the window, the city danced around her in squares of abstraction. Concrete edifices gave way to stone buildings. All was lit. Oblong, square and rectangular yellow and bluish windows stuck fingers and tongues at her as intrusive as every built-up city pokes at you. It was pleasantly colourful although anything but restful.

IN THE EARLY hours of the morning she half-woke. Her pillow was twisted and bunched beneath her black, frizzy hair. A tug of war had left both hair and pillow in a hopeless pile. She had fought something in her sleep which had faded and was gone even as she woke. No comfort, she thought bitterly, to be had in dreaming.

She got up and looked in the mirror. What a ghostly face. And her eyes were mere slits. She froze at the uncertain light coming in through the window; at the dim haziness which illumined objects eerily immobile. She seemed a bizarre creature, the only living thing in the room.

The city, so gigantic and sprawling, had troubled

her in the night. The screeching and braking, although many floors down, rose up and entered her subconscious.

ELIZABETH FELT her life ruled by city anonymity.

She needed badly the pleasantry of nature.

She was alone in an anonymous hotel room. Her night-thoughts were dire; loneliness draped around her shoulders.

As she smoothed the sheets and pulled the duvet back over her, she took comfort in her memories of the waters surrounding the island of Mull on the West Coast of Scotland where she was born. Thoughts of rising and settling waves soothed her.

She remembered the sea's tranquillity and its silver shining largesse, though she knew the ocean could suddenly rise in mercurial agitation. Turning the duvet away from her face, she pictured how the green waves spumed and curled the white water. Never did the tranquil silvery sheen last for long.

No, seascapes and landscapes were forceful. And each element—whether water, air, or earth; whether assembled into a lake; or trees grouped in earthen, shadowy frames to veil or hide—wanted her to respond.

Her eyes widened. She got up and swung the

sheets and duvet aside. She saw herself in the mirror and straightened her shoulders.

BREAKFAST

Elizabeth was dressed in a neat, lady-like suit and her frilly, ruffled blue blouse. She fancied coffee and toast after tossing so long in her sleep.

She entered the breakfast room early. There were not many people present. She surveyed the room that was laid out with cups, water glasses, cutlery and plates. Only one other table in a corner was occupied, where two men leaned intently towards one another, conversing rapidly.

The dark-suited man was gesturing towards an overly long and broad case at his feet. He shoved at it with his toes, but it must have been heavy because it didn't move. The man from the Middle East—his robes of white billowed out every time he moved and he was neatly bearded—smiled suddenly. He looked down and seemed to approve of whatever was packed into the case.

The waiter hovered. Not over Elizabeth, but over those intensely preoccupied men. They started up surprised and waved him away, getting up, straining to appear casual. The Arab man lifted the oblong case—he had to retrieve it with both hands—and walked out. The other man followed him. But Elizabeth saw how a flash of money unobtrusively stuffed into an envelope came to be pocketed. This was done in a flash by the dark-suited Brit.

Quick as a shower of rain, both the men strode away and out the door of the breakfast room.

Elizabeth was by now imbibing her eagerly awaited second cup of coffee. She doused it with a liberal splurge of milk. She dug into her Eggs Benedict.

The waiter crossed the room and hovered over her. In order to deflect his interest, she said, "I wonder what could induce these well-dressed visitors that had such a copious breakfast over there, to bring such a heavy case with them while they were eating. You must, as a grand hotel, have places to put guests' luggage!"

"Oh we do, we do," he said, removing her half-eaten egg and replenishing her coffee, "but some guests are never parted from their shiny treasures, their silver triggers and swords—their teddy-bear luxuries." And he laughed.

It was then she spied hanging on the wall an elaborate abstract painting. She was stupefied to find her father's work so far from home and prominently displayed.

This one was a picture of pounding waves, but in an exciting panoply of red, gold, vermilion and lemon yellow cascading as if the waters were coming straight at the viewer and would envelop and engulf. The salty drops were a vivid blue, sprayed as randomly as surf. And the green swards of grass near the bottom enlivened only a smidgen of the lower frame, a breathing landline, startling the sea and motioning that this is the end of the swirling waters. The grass was the shore.

The painting illustrated the power of the sea. The liveliness was there, but also the threat.

The waters danced in vivid colour and their message was to entice—and to raise the idea of casting caution to the wind—this very element, wind, that swept the sea in agitation. The message was both to enjoy and to beware.

The painting outmanoeuvred reality; it spoke beyond explicit representation.

Elizabeth was left pondering her feelings: these vivid lines made her heart pound.

Her father had been an artist. He had struggled

to express in colour and shapes his belief that art reached beyond the real world, became engrained in the blood and, indeed, made more reachable what was in the mind. He never thought anybody remained untouched by startling, abstract, and even emotional plotting. He wanted his painting removed from the concrete, from hard and fast reality. He tried to enliven the imagination through forms and colours, but imagination was hard to capture. There was always that moment of interchange between those who looked at pictures and those who created them. No matter what the aims, viewer and creator had to come together, had to share innovation and this had to be defined by the artwork.

Victor had bequeathed to Elizabeth strong attitudes and money enough to be independent. He had also imbued her with the desire to travel.

He was a high-brow German and she found herself straddling cultures—not always easy.

For long moments, Elizabeth lost all sense of her surroundings.

Her father had fallen in love with a woman strikingly well-mannered but with unruly hair and Scottish tartan taste in dresses. They had met while Fiona stood in front of one of his paintings that seemed to spray spewing waves at viewers.

Love was an odd thing, bringing opposites together, merging lives. And Elizabeth was its product, which she accepted, dipping joyfully into crannies unexplored and unearthing clues where these were only suggested. Her father had incorporated hints and visions in his work, but also left questions unanswered. This was the magic of his paintings. He portrayed the abstract but the abstract merged with emotions.

The natural landscape of the Scottish islands championed the caprice of weather and unexpected moods. It induced feelings when the mountains were dreich and happiness when shadows and sun prevailed. Elizabeth's father had tried capturing the natural scenes, but abstracted them. He made representation become reaction and this became fundamentally significant to those he had intrigued by his use of shape and colours.

Her mother, too, had contributed to her being wary of commonplace, easy answers. At heart an individual who went her own way, she had instilled in her daughter that there was nothing wrong in growing up pursuing ideas that find a place in the mind.

Elizabeth sat very still, almost as if she were alone in the room. Mull, the Scottish island, had risen from primeval volcanoes, many hills crowned with ancient lore—even dragons were reputed to live there.

Mull was a strong island, repulsing the strong

winds and spuming waves that came from as far away as America. The hills were in stark contrast with the island's sumptuous clouds, variable in movement, driven sometimes to colossal white, wavy, pleated heights.

Elizabeth so cherished her reverie, that for a moment she was at a loss about where she was.

She was living one moment, but recalling another. Her awareness was stretching. She looked up briefly, but once again dived into island imagery.

The cloudy ornaments of the islands were often luxurious, luminous, pearling structures threaded with dark hues. Where a watery sun chose to shine through them, they were glancing white-rimmed bodies, cloaked in backlit beauty. These spirals of contrast were ever moving, making the hills shine or topping them in gloom. The weather and the mountains gave the island the feel of imminent doom or happiness.

This homeland was startling, and it was the reason for Elizabeth's singular desire, so very strong, to want to explore what landscapes meant.

She was touched to the marrow by art.

And she had made up her mind to explore; to see how this affected her. Henry Hoare the Magnificent still survived in Wiltshire, at Stourhead.

But her next stop would be to visit that beautiful river statue in Somerset House.

It was, after all, why she had come to this big city. London was so variable but all of it depended on the River Thames.

She waved to the waiter as she left, her mind still on her family.

Her father had been an unexpected quirky addition to Fiona's island life. He had been a man of contrasting imagination to that of the down-to-earth Fiona. Elizabeth's mother was always practical, despite cultivating outlandish dress. It was her beneficial habits that helped nurture just how her father adjusted to island life, sharpening his eccentricities. Fiona was a good choice for him and he appreciated it.

But her partner was a brooding, melancholy German refugee, too old to care long for their love child, legitimized in the nick of time. He had died too soon, leaving Elizabeth's mother bereft.

However, her father lived on in the incredible structure, colour, and emotion of his pictures.

ELIZABETH STARED at her replica in the elevator's mirror. Her frizzy black hair was contained in an Alice-band to keep her forehead free. She wore bright pink lipstick. It livened up her blue frilly blouse and contrasted well with her demure black suit of clothes.

At least the waiter had taken note. He had treated her as if she mattered. She wondered, idly, if she had made a diverting impression, too, on those very mundane and international men who were such good talkers, concentrating all the time and not even able to relax over breakfast.

Surely they deserved some explosive chilli pepper with their toast!

She was prone to liking disruption and she recalled how she grew up, donning fanciful costumes and roles, whatever she chose. She rarely cried, though there had been challenging times too, which she had surmounted. But she had never found anyone who shared her interests or truly loved her enough to be a companion.

She thought again of her mother. Fiona's beauty and waywardness had some time later persuaded an aristocrat to marry her and her second marriage had given Elizabeth a half-sister, Mhairi. Her mother had treasured her only child by a war-stricken German, and mourned his love. But she bowed to the happy fate of a second marriage on Mull and her next child. Her new marriage gave her renewed sustenance and the care she badly needed after Victor's death. She adjusted happily to the love of a Scotsman who owned an estate. She had Mhairi and much work to do. Elizabeth and Mhairi were close, being half-sisters, though Mhairi had grown to be different in temperament, happier with a settled life. The half-sisters had made their home on the tip of Mull, on the estate of Dunmoray where Mhairi was dutifully in charge. And Elizabeth carried the mésalliance of hope and despair that was engrained in her German name, Hammerstein, to adulthood.

HOLIDAY PLANS

The glass of beer had a rich, foamy crest and the brew underneath was rich, dark bronze. The anglophile German inspector of police, Horatio Queberon, raised his glass, toasting the Elbe River, rapidly flowing north past him. Just below, the Kornhaus restaurant terrace was still empty. He was alone and contemplating getting away from it all. In the next few days he planned to leave his home town of Dessau and travel incognito to Britain.

Nothing like leaving everything behind, he was thinking, all that rot of endless paperwork, the marshalling of police officers, or even his dutiful turning up at the police headquarters. He could feel his muscles relaxing because he would soon be gone.

Usually so very conscientious, his first day of holidays tended to be flippant and carefree.

So he raised his glass at the river before him. This was the timeless, broad and fast-moving Elbe River, bearing its currents in tiny rivulets and flexing its waves. In spring, the river was slightly swollen from melting snow that fed from its origins. But that was far away and he was basking in the first early warm days the river seemed to bring with it. Trees were budding and covered in a light green. He could see them close to him beyond the terrace where he was sitting and even further down the slope across the river.

He was enjoying his meal of potatoes, spinach, and sausages. The Kornhaus had its origins in the now much vaunted Bauhaus movement, but Queberon was just basking in the first hints of spring weather and letting all serious ideas slide.

He liked the semi-wild running currents, a splashing wave or two, and the bend before him of the river. These upper waters were hiding the tumultuous strength of the Elbe which had come a long way and was going even further. As he sat there, his mind emptied.

"Enjoying the view," commented a fellow officer who had entered the Kornhaus to have some lunch. One of the police officers that Queberon had so hoped to get away from.

Queberon exhibited, briefly, a furrowed and disgruntled frown, then quickly changed this into a show of uncommon friendliness. "Have an off-duty beer on me and don't even mention law and order. I suggest you behave like you've never even seen the statute books! I'm on my holiday and whatever you say, I promise to forget."

His fellow officer sat down. "I understand you're flying abroad. Examining landscape gardens for pleasure over in England. Landscape gardens that actually surround you everywhere here!"

Queberon took the point. "No, this is not new. Even such an incredibly uninformed, unread, insomniac like you, would welcome restful sleep in a green and pleasant land. I'm exploring what's there in Britain that's inspired what's here.

"Or, if you like plain language, I'm keen on why the Dessau-Woerlitz landscape gardens creator liked the idea of British landscape gardens. I wonder why we have a Pantheon and a village church overlooking our landscape gardens—I like links, and I am going to meander around 'til I'm drowsy with being well informed. And walking lakes and trees is far removed from investigating crime!"

"Ha, dear fellow criminologist! Deny that Britain is proud of inviting the gods to enliven its waters and woods. You'll thrive in the supernatural—and vegetate in surroundings that spell out how far you're liberated from dykes and canals here. They were deeply dug with a design in mind. Who'll tell you in such a quick time as holidays allow, anything about rivers, lakes, temples and views over to this and that—and in closed-mouthed Britain!"

The younger officer laughed.

Since it was his turn Queberon dug in and said, "You're right, I want to find out about design. But design is based on ideas—and that, my friend, believe it or not, was the treasure trove of British Liberty which inspired that digging of lakes and canals that made the eighteenth-century Prince of Anhalt-Dessau happy. So there. He wanted to raise his own modern banner. And plant and build—or should I say: hide in low and exotic branches buildings of fairytale character."

"No doubt you earn titles both as inquisitive detective and inspector—even on your holidays—and how could anyone deny you your police badge though you may be on your day off! It's a good thing I don't know exactly where you're headed." The chatty younger officer buried his nose in the fresh and foaming glass of beer he was presented with through Queberon's graceful sign language.

"Stourhead is where I'm going, that early eighteenth-century landscape garden, since you want to be my confessor," said Queberon. "It has a Pantheon, a River God, and a Tower of Liberty. And plenty to think about."

The beer was good, up to both their exacting standards.

The younger officer meditated, then asked, "Landscape gardens must have something in common. Certainly rivers. They need lots of water, if Dessau is anything to go by."

"There's all that practical shaping, yes. But why these gardens display temples is another thing. The views are so grand—you see the rising Pantheon, the homes of gods and goddesses over water formed to lakes and they are revealed sitting high as you clear a path. Grand domed structures. They harbour religions and supernatural beings inside." And with a challenging look, Queberon raised his eyebrows.

"I hope that is not what you're longing to see— all that energy the Greek and Roman statues keep hidden. Better to appreciate how memorials are placed—I grant you, always distant over water so you see them, but can't get there easily. The Dessau-Woerlitz gardens give you enough on that score— their sightlines are more copious than the paths."

"I think that's why I'm taking this jaunt," replied Queberon. "I'm revelling in gardens of grand shapes that have a tradition of their own. They spread along the Thames and they spread to the many countries that wanted to fashion nature as thought-provoking—Dessau among the very first—and they make you think. And one of the focal points is to think on why we still have gods and goddesses. Is it very wise to journey such a long way only to watch what sightlines reveal? To stand agog before that picture of the Parthenon, glorious with its dome and grand rectangle, on a hill above?

"The Stourhead one stands out against its trees. The Palladian Bridge seems to lead to it above the lake which is only partially shown, but silvery and grey, below it. The Dessau Parthenon is dominant too. But it sits on a dam above a widening canal, and a bridge honouring the golden rays of the sun on the next watery canal. These are all revelations—these are all constructions we come upon. They are man-made. These very silent things whisper: Remember, you are part of us."

The young officer looked out over the Elbe. "I'm learning. The next time I'll see more! But seriousness aside, let's eat!" And with that they both turned their minds to the plates in front of them.

LEFT ALONE after the young officer's departure, Queberon watched the rippling river swiftly run downstream.

In contrast to the river's galloping pace, he mused that for once there were no longer ten-thousand things for him to do right away. Still, a sense of melancholy lingered—for his house was empty; no welcome and cheery talk. He was still burdened with bachelorhood.

The trees, newly green, concurred in sympathy. But they were across the river, far away.

Queberon decided to walk along the dam of the Elbe River that had wild nature on one side and the greenery of the extended landscape garden on the other. It was designed as a twist of lakes and deliberately placed patches of trees. As he walked, he soon fell into a nebulous haze, a dreaming sense of unreality. He wandered far on the high sloping top of the dam, letting his eye catch both the flood plain and the many temples built to connect with the sky. He gazed at the lovely, emerging spring landscape, but then his mind went to one of the places that often attracted his thoughts.

He visualized the bridge that so often entered his consciousness unbidden but emblematic. A bridge suspended between two rocky heights above a canal in the Dessau landscape garden. He had traversed it many times and now it invaded his mind as a confrontation with his past: it accentuated what was his perennial puzzle.

This bridge, he felt, was the flimsiest of laced-together planks and anyone who dared to cross it risked falling into the watery depths of the wide and murky canal.

He had to find balance. He was no longer young and wanted a new start. He felt as though he was rocking back and forth on that precarious bridge.

He remembered another encounter, that very white, angelic sculpture that was at the end of a tunnel when you had to decide which road to take. You had to choose. You couldn't go any further. It was meant as an encounter to think on which road to take. A fork in the road. One or the other. The Angel of Destiny awaiting. Queberon shook himself. Better not to think that way on holiday.

THE RIVER GOD THAMES

Along the Thames the London Eye winked its circular gyrations, bright and ominous, turning like the wheel of fortune as it rose, revolving, above the river waters.

Elizabeth walked from the River Thames to meander in the courtyard of Somerset House. She viewed the waterworks that threw many jets upwards, none of them contemplating the same height. Each one seemed to run vertically to its highest position, then subsided and became next to nothing. It was a miraculous play of watery jet streams. Redolent of life with all its mishaps, it rang the variations of the moon, three dark nights, low, not to be seen, and then a glimmering light rising regularly to the fullness of the glowing moon. And there it was again, the white full moon.

In its monthly glory the moon would be encountered again and again, rising in the lunar month, each lunar year. The watery jet streams were glinting, yet they too rippled in dark channels. They rose and fell.

She looked about her. And saw this place's many watery predecessors. Above the ground and below it were London's many rivers. But she wanted especially to see the Thames again because the landscape garden at Stourhead—already at the time of its inception—had gained inspiration from thoughts and buildings erected in central London.

The great architect, William Chambers, had built Somerset House for the Navy, so it was naturally filled with watery symbols and seemed the natural starting point for learning the meaning of rivers. She would start here, like any child, dousing herself in the lore and stories supplied by the ancients.

Elizabeth knew that even if she appeared an isolated woman, she was not abandoned in the kinship that stories gave her. On every corner there was a whispering of myths, of legends, of wind and rain, of the deeds of the gods, even stones casting lively shadows, and the trees too shook with vigour in spring, murmuring amongst themselves.

From stories, she knew that in the ancient world rivers were revered. They were as alive as she was. In one of the best known myths, Daphne ran away from an enamoured Apollo. As she fled, she appealed to her father, the River God Peneos, who turned Daphne into a laurel tree.

Enchanted, Elizabeth walked in the morning sunshine. This time of year all was charmingly vivid, the light illuminating each crevice and cobblestone until the ground was like a woven carpet. The water glistened and darkened where the fountains left puddles on the ground. What joy to know so much from centuries past had survived.

But she did have an ulterior motive. She wanted to find the monument Chambers made for the River God Thames. She was taking her walk this morning in round-about curves, as if she were entering another tier of thinking.

To her delight, she ended her walk around the courtyard with the reclining figure of a bearded man, lying on his side and holding a cornucopia. This was the figure of Old Father Thames she had come to see.

Father Thames had been completed at the same time as Somerset House and he echoed the heady waters numerous sailors had ploughed through on their voyages when they came to do business at last at these Naval Headquarters.

Elizabeth Hammerstein stopped in front of this well-proportioned figure because this was the emblem she wanted to consider before going on to Stourhead.

The figureheads of rivers told the stories of the bounty and safe harbour of running and rippling waters. They were both arteries of navigation and means to keep the fields green and grazed. Rivers were sacred and celebrated. Old Father Thames was a water deity, his flowing hair attesting to the swirls and currents running and twisting in eddies, but also renewal and growth as in his cornucopia.

"Rivers bring so many things, the good and the bad, inundations of fertility and devastating floods," murmured Elizabeth.

The Thames being one of the mightiest rivers and a prerogative of monarchs would help her understand, she meditated, how homage mattered in the springs and the first flow of that other river, the River Stour. The Thames had been important early on. It was easier to transport people and goods on this waterway. Easier than the lumpy and wayward paths when carriages went off roads frequently enough. And the Thames had not been without its special folklore and myths. Its windings had paid tribute to sea-creatures rising from the depths, in reality beyond the mere actions of humans. Stories anchor happenings. They bequeath them to subsequent generations.

Rivers gushed downwards from sparkling

springs. Nymphs and River Gods were put in place to heed this remarkable happening in lush valleys from the times of the Greeks onwards. Perhaps it was this veneration for water and quiet shade that led to the sacred grove. "The sacred spring was one with the watery ground, but also gave rise to gods of place," said Elizabeth, musing to herself, but also having found her starting point.

"Hercules broke one of the horns of the river god and that is why, in the strange mutation these stories have, the River God carries a horn of plenty. He glories in it. The cornucopia is rich in flowers and plant life, containing the source of life as rivers do when they are rich in soil and inundate their flood plain. All rivers bring forth the waters that vegetation needs for growth and loveliness. They cause flowers to bloom."

Her mind raced with ideas. Now she had come face to face with this elegant bronze and the optimistic character of a River God decked in flowers, she would be happy to see the River God in Stourhead. It helped her appreciate what was coming. But the River God Stour was not as opulent as Father Thames. He was a fierce god, and pointed upwards in his white spuming, rising, statuesque sheen while forever master in his underground cave.

As she stood there lost in thought, she seemed to hear an almighty outcry from some tall and muscular men. It assaulted her ears. They were chasing after a grey veiled, oddly grey clothed, seemingly nineteenth-century woman. The lady appeared like a phantom amongst the blue and energetic group of policemen.

To Elizabeth this was an hallucination—but it droned in her ear. She shook her head. She wanted rid of ladies who appeared so uninvited to sit or run too close to her. But she looked anyway. She was brave enough to appreciate ghosts.

These policemen were very odd, she thought. Their uniforms were out-of-date. Their commands were echoes ricocheting from buildings. If she listened closely, no sound was there at all.

And yet, words, make-shift, like traffic noises amplified by the courtyard were to be heard. To her they made some sense, but she knew how the smallest thing amplified into meaning for her. She was, after all, sensitive to shifts even in shadows.

Voices boomed like a ship's horn and garbled near and from afar. They shouted breathlessly—and wanted to know which way this grey-looking lady had gone; none of the policemen in their now black, now blue flickering uniforms had found the grey lady. The alien woman had vanished, elevated to nothingness, right in their midst.

After these policemen quite suddenly disappeared—they now seemed weightless—what emerged was ominous indeed.

The grey lady set foot right in front of Elizabeth and whispered to her as if she wanted her undivided attention. The grey lady seemed to be there, albeit she seemed only passing, crowding in on her, as the old lady had done in the aeroplane.

Elizabeth glanced about, but could not, for the life of her, pin down that flickering, grey-clothed lady. In the blink of an eye she was gone.

Elizabeth saw nothing but rustic stones and doorways.

And nothing moved. The statue of the long-haired River God was silent and his cornucopia remained stationary like it always had.

However, an odd bright light hovered around the statue.

Words reached her, whispered in loud then soft screeching tones as they echoed along the rustic stones. *Be watchful in Stourhead.*

Elizabeth felt apprehension. Trouble was brewing, but she could not pinpoint the when, the where, or the how.

Only the River God, with his statuesque silence, gazed disembodied into the future. Or so it seemed.

RAILWAY JOURNEY

Pondering strange illusions and ominous messages, Elizabeth stood on a moderately busy platform. The train she wanted to catch was for Bath. She had asked her friend Rosalinde de Ludewig to meet her when the train arrived and take her to Stourhead by car.

They had shared the four years at Girton, meeting in the first year in the lonely reaches of the Cambridge Library. Meeting again and again in such a quiet place and recognizing their mutual immersion in books, their eyes had met. Stacks of books had hid their faces, but they peeked around at each other and then introduced themselves.

Elizabeth had retained her secret passion for the frivolous and entertaining with its tall stories that had so amused Rosalinde. Her friend had relished exorbitant tales. And so Elizabeth told her about Kelpies in Scotland rising out of the waters—and drowning those enticed to ride them. Elizabeth told her the stories of seals and how they cast off their beautiful furry skins. And thereafter the poor seals had to live human lives. And all because a starry-eyed seal had fallen in love. In human form these seals did chores and were wise—until they yearned for the sea, the sea waves spuming in transparent whites and the ocean depths lurking far from shore. Then they searched for cast-off skins, deposited in hidden trunks or forgotten in wardrobes—and, for all the years spent on land, waved greetings from the sea.

Elizabeth's stories stirred Rosalinde, and the pair created one of those bonds which survive upheavals. Whenever they met—and that was now infrequent—they had told each other the truth no matter how awful this was. They would meet once more—and soon now. Elizabeth was on her way to Bath.

IN THE LONG succession of carriages, Elizabeth settled into a pleasant seat next to the window. She was travelling at the time of day when there were few passengers. Hopefully she could spread out her things and relax. She had consciously chosen the back of the train, one of the last carriages. The route was full of hills and vales and she would let the verdant early green of spring cheer her soul.

But as chance would have it, the nearly empty compartment at the end of the train was filling. The man who took the seat opposite her nodded a curt hello and remained silent.

What Elizabeth couldn't know, was that this man who stepped firmly into those seemingly empty compartments was trading on being alone just as she was. And he was journeying to Stourhead, but heaven help her finding that out.

To break the ice, Elizabeth raised her eyes to ask where, perchance, he was going?

"Bath—and not to heaven," he answered smoothly and with a quirky irony, looking at her orderly dress and habitual tidiness.

"Sounds like you're no angel," she laughed in response, thinking nothing of it but silly banter.

"I don't believe in angels' wings, and certainly nothing beyond the physical," he countered, and produced a sardonic smile.

Elizabeth felt her hackles rise. He might be one of today's finance experts, so used to finding fulfilment in procuring money. Certainly he was dressed expensively, a sure indication of higher income, but his manner was devilish in his condescension. He definitely looked satanic.

In truth, he was as hard as flint. He had had the twisted upbringing of parents vying for his attention as an only son. This brought the belief of his being superior in all ways. He always championed nothing but himself even as a young child. But it did not help moderation toward others. He picked people up and let them drop.

His machinations were centred on Stourhead at present. The front as financier was one of his many disguises.

Stabbing into the blue, Elizabeth remarked: "But angels know exactly how to invent things to beautiful effect. They know things inside out. They know how to manage finances as well as a fluttery soul," and she smiled beatifically.

He put his suitcase above him on the rack. Then he looked down on her. "Angels are nothing but figments of the imagination. Try something material like wearing glasses: the more you see, the less you're inclined to imagine."

Angels were the very thing that needed her defence, Elizabeth thought suddenly.

"Imagination can lead you to better things than mere materialism can … you, yourself, may not need more than the basic facts! But try novels that have the habit of telling beautiful truths or music like that of Haydn or Beethoven made to rouse or calm your soul. If you have a soul, that is."

"I don't, and I don't particularly want one," he answered, grimacing.

She tried looking out the window. The budding trees were exploding. Nature and life were exuberant.

"You must be on top of your art, to be so confident," she said.

"Nothing like money. I'm with one of the best hedge funds, a man of means. And my clients are utterly grateful," he pronounced.

"Well, you're going in the wrong direction," said Elizabeth.

She had been right to think him intolerable.

Granted, she had started this sparring. But he seemed easily needled; bankers usually tried to be more urbane.

She raised the stakes. "Bath is full of magical half-circles, if not circles, and they were intentionally conceived to make you think of Rome or Druids, not brick or mortar. Even now they exude their richness. What is an obelisk, but a sign of resurrection? There is a magnificent obelisk in Queen's Square. It and Bath's many crescents were constructed in the eighteenth century. That was above all the century of reason, yet they lived visibly in places that pleaded the opposite."

He was suddenly charming. He bent towards her, more flirtatious than most. His face was handsome: splendid, convincing dark eyes, pale but golden skin, a hawkish nose, but a chin that balanced fierceness with capability.

Elizabeth was not taken in; her Isle of Mull grittiness took the high road. She shot him a disparaging glance.

"John Wood the Elder, if you know him, and a fine man he was too, floats just out of reach. Were you an architect you'd love his pagan ways. Even if you were an apostate, you'd be heaped with the belief that some things were beyond us, flat earth plus black holes. He designed the first square, the Queen's Square, from which all the other crescents that make Bath so unique took inspiration.

"I believe in ghosts," she added firmly and she looked at him provokingly, purposely at her most irritating. She was thinking back just now on her eerie experience in the Dessau landscape gardens where her former investigation of early eighteenth-century gardens had all started with the aristocrats Henriette von Lippe-Weisenfels and Louise von Anhalt-Dessau. They had appeared to her in ghostly shapes. And this was where she had almost drowned and was only just saved by a German inspector of police, Horatio Queberon.

The gold-chained, dark-suited man moved abruptly, took his hat off, and said, "Let's agree to disagree. My name is James Owen. As you guessed, I'm a successful financier."

He had changed tactics.

"And I'm Professor Hammerstein, an academic," she countered. She wished to draw even, and, she then added, not won over so easily, "committed to themes more difficult than mere theorizing, namely exact and even spiritual explanation."

He sat down and looked exactly just as he wished, posing as the successful fund manager.

It was at this point she leaned forward in her seat to judge him up close. It seemed to her that here, rather than just another difficult man, was a man who was worthy of interest.

He was not much older than she was, careworn despite his youth, trussed up in clothes that were formal, almost Victorian. For all his modern views, she could tell, looking closer, that he was composed of ill-fitting parts.

She was stuck with him until Bath. It gave her some satisfaction that he must listen, confined to the railway compartment as he was. She began her explanation of landscape gardens.

But she was startled to see he was interested. More than that, he seemed to come to fresh attention.

Elizabeth decided to risk exposing him to some of her thinking on the subject, puzzling all the while why he seemed so receptive. Was he pretending, in what seemed to her an indirect way, to gain her favour? Or did he want to gain knowledge on Stourhead itself?

"It may seem far-fetched to you, but our nature is our landscape and be it either in one of London's deprived areas, or some grand castle of Elizabethan times, it forms how you are more than your DNA. I will point out to you that the landscape I am going to has been designed for a purpose. Stourhead is not simply a lake with some obscure temples hovering around in it, made for amusement centuries ago. As visitors descend the valley, the trees, the lake, the deities take over. Whoever descends finds relationships, the more involved they become, the more the spirits breathe to envelop them, much more than normally deemed possible."

"Are you headed toward Stourhead?" he asked. "Then you might explain to me how the ancient church and the pantheon of gods assembled can make their peace in such surroundings."

Elizabeth crossed her legs. They were long and elegant. Her hair was in its customary frizzy mode. She now wore a red rose scarf, left on over her light green pullover and charcoal skirt. Her black coat with fake fur collar was on the hook behind her. Her hat was out of fashion, but its cloche shape, although hanging with the coat, repeated the rose pattern in faded blooms to the side, in the same red, and buds as well as full-blown flowers.

When she spoke, it was with the authority of one well-versed in the history of Stourhead.

"Down the valley, you see nothing but nicely arranged ornamental buildings. They grace the incline, and are pretty things belonging to another age.

"Stourhead gardens instigate presences. The most obvious is that of the gods. Some of which are Greek in origin; others, Roman versions.

"What's more," Elizabeth went on, "how do you reconcile the very long view up the valley, capped by Alfred's Tower, Hoare's ode to British Liberty, with the assembly of the gods' habitations, Apollo's shrine and the temple to all the pagan gods? Hoare was obviously thinking how much he valued the intervention of the powerful gods and goddesses he assembled. In a sense he transcended the centuries. And what is more, his life is related to the activities of the gods. Everywhere in this landscape there are relationships. And, I may add," she gave him a hard stare, "very little materialism."

James Owen said nothing.

IN BATH

Rosalinde de Ludewig was pacing the platform, recalling the young, feisty undergraduates they had been. Elizabeth, with her island upbringing, was disconcerting at first, but grew closer as they became more sympathetic to each other—and more audacious to others.

Elizabeth tied men into knots. Laughing, she subsequently undid men's predicaments, like the sailor she was. She was used to ropes and fancy handiwork. Thus, to use her nautical language, she slipped whatever the moorings were. In effect, she never let men get the better of her. But in this way she also missed precious opportunities to be loved.

Ah, there she was: Elizabeth, somewhat older, but energetic as always, hat clamped to her head, coat wrapped around, face eagerly searching the straggly multitude that met the train, suitcase in hand. And there was Rosalinde waiting, stepping as fast as her heels allowed, to embrace her long-lost friend.

They had not seen each other for years, but living in different parts of the country had not altered their affection for each other. Rosalinde wore a smart suit in deep blues. She had her own antiques shop and was making a modest profit.

They were chattering avidly when they both caught sight of the Victorian figure of James Owen. Rosalinde turned swiftly. She felt a frisson and revulsion travel up her spine.

She said, "Look over there, discreetly of course; you will see a complete contradiction in terms. On the outside a calmly collected man our own age, but beneath it all a hedonist despite being in Victorian dress! A man—over there, look—who believes only in money, and glories only in the moment.

"I remember," she said, "he came into my shop and bought a landscape painting done in the style of the picturesque school, the lightning flashing vigorously over rocks and cascading water, all gloom and dark skies, except for a ray of sunshine breaking through clouds and illuminating the entranced wayfarer taking in that dramatic scene."

James Owen, the man who had come into her

shop, was now walking down the platform away from them. He was vanishing down the platform.

"That man fascinated me. I fell for him badly."

Rosalinde had a furrowed brow and a sharp intake of breath. She continued in a sharp tone. "Then after a short time, suddenly, he spoke to me in completely dismissive terms. He wanted to return to his agenda of making money, without the endless distraction of a fashionable woman and her fashionable trade in antiques. These provided only a moderate income. He said as much. He had a devilish laugh. He was so dismissive of me. He said I was all emotional and wrong."

And she went on, giving Elizabeth a most ironic and puzzled look: "But he wanted to buy that one picture he had seen in my store anyway. He talked of it reminding him of foolhardy, black-and-white approaches to life. It cost him a pretty penny.

"He told me there is mystery in the dark sides of life; so he's going to hang it on the wall to tell again and again of how the sudden descent of forks of lightning can illuminate everything. Striking insights by forked lightning, he said. Dark and Light are best seen from afar; they are bitter opposites. And I am King of the Jungle, like the onlooker, seeing landscapes plunged into lightning, but not in any way risking myself. This is what he wanted, viewing happenings only from afar.

"And he believes in nothing that is sublime or beautiful—even though that is what the painting seeks to convey, what the picturesque was saying when the landscape was immersed by such terror. And to see it, as it becomes conscious, is to feel the terror that landscapes can produce. You are confronted. The desire to let the painting become a reflection of your thinking and emotions as you take in life is envisioned in this picture. These picturesque paintings are there to enter your heart, make you reflect on your life, as participant not as onlooker.

"Owen missed the point. He likes to be the controller pointing to the scene. He likes to see the turmoil in others, but he himself remains untouchable. He says the money that he gains, in the end, is all that matters. Even if others are cast into pain, emotion and despair.

"He misses the point and makes himself distant and frozen, above any influence that anyone has, above all care and ..." She was angry now, but she held to her views because she had long studied the why and what-for of paintings. She added, "How you manage emotions is crucial and important and the opposite to what he thinks—looking at the picture he bought tells you so. You are to reflect, feel that storm, not distance yourself."

"I've just met him on the train," said Elizabeth

when Rosalinde paused long enough. She gave a short laugh to ease the sudden turmoil. "I tried to convince him that Stourhead was more than a pretty place full of temples."

She turned to her friend. "Remember our fantastical tales? No one could emulate us! It appears to me that these sedate, picture-postcard images of Stourhead reflect nothing but unreal serenity. And avoid all emotional scrutiny. People glory in the never-changing landscape. They don't pause and take in their feelings. But, actually, it tells a more turbulent story if the gods come alive.

"Hoare gave them a sedate presence as statues, but they can stir into action. These gods and goddesses are meant to confront us spiritually and encourage us to try to emulate their virtues.

"The gods and goddesses of the Pantheon display artfulness, but they have powers that can descend on the material world. And I don't mean just the jiggling of nerves culminating in modern romance—which we can quite do without."

They were equals. They talked about their deep beliefs and what made them uneasy. And, finally, they walked together down the platform, dodging the busy people bustling about and opened the doors to Rosalinde's comfortable old Mercedes.

. . .

"I LIVE OVER THE SHOP, so to speak," said Rosalinde. "And firstly I'll show you this, my shop, where I'm proprietor! And I'll show you my hidden treasures, some relating to your current favourite landscape garden, you'll be happy to know."

They alighted to find a jumble of many things, all from different centuries, some bright and ready to be displayed as treasure found in Bath. Some were taken to the corners of the room towards the back, away from the bay windows. Only where good lighting shone on them were these revealed as special. Deposited in nooks and crooks, they seemed only forgotten goods.

Elizabeth was immediately struck by a centuries-old portrait of a man on a horse, a copy no doubt, of a striking youth in a formidable jacket and streaming hair, but in command of it all. It was an etching, by an unknown artist, of the young Henry Hoare.

Elizabeth was startled to find such a portrait, but it was no more than to be expected in Bath. She admired her friend in gathering such significant objects for the antiquarian trade.

"That's the banker," explained Rosalinde, "he was so tired in London, that all he wanted was a retreat. So he built one. He was privileged. He lent money to so many, even Charles Hamilton of Painshill. That was what probably inspired the blue

Turkish tent which is no longer there in Stourhead," she added casually.

"You know more than I think," said Elizabeth, "but Henry Hoare was also interested in politics. He was greatly torn by all William Pitt, the prime minister at the time, and his successors, did. Hoare minded all the wars Great Britain got involved in fighting. He liked peace better and hated making money out of people who were at each other's throats."

"Mind you," Rosalinde countered, "he was soon above money matters, though he was not spared sorrow; he had two daughters and only one of them, Ann, survived. The other one, Susanna, was memorialized in a statue in the Parthenon.

"But do let's get onto other subjects. I'd like to find out more about Mull, about Mhairi, and dare I say it, about you."

Elizabeth murmured, "I'm still single, but it has its good points; I'm very much my own woman. Mhairi wants me to settle down, be like her, full to the brim with domestic bliss. She loves it at the family estate in Dunmoray. Found a partner she's happy with, Colin, and, although overwhelmed by chores, is content to stay put. In contrast, I'm restless, glad to be on the move."

They mounted the stairs in companionship, not at all different from the friendship they had enjoyed in Cambridge. They felt as young and inventive now as they had been then. They seemed closer, even, as, moving about in Bath, they could look back at such a mutually beneficial and after so many years, long history. Together they talked about their discoveries and possible futures. Both were alert and sure of their continued will to make their own mark.

"You'll bring out the connection to virtues and the spiritual side that's there in the landscape garden, mute but present," ventured Rosalinde. "Not what everyone wants to realize, no doubt, but it emphasizes how landscape gardens create an active emotional life when you engage with them. Your interpretation says these gardens provoke involvement, not just leisure and passing through. It's the antithesis to James Owen and his ilk."

Inside Rosalinde's comfortable flat, the curtains were drawn, and a fire took the chill off the still cool, but beginning-to-be-in-leaf time. The chairs were chintzy and the sofa an affair of colourful cushions and patterned good taste.

Scones were waiting.

"I do miss the sea around Mull, the tempestuous blue and the threatening grey clouds. I love the wind skating cold over the mountains, but I like travelling to the South—and meeting old friends!" said Elizabeth. She settled on the inviting sofa.

"There is much and little to be said about my recent adventures," she mused. "I was most often in Germany. In a landscape garden that survived over the centuries but was also once located in the former GDR. I visited one of the first landscape gardens there that was patterned after the English ones, in Dessau. While I was there, it turned out that the gardens were heavily used for criminal activities. I had the companionship of one of the police detective-inspectors. He was an anglophile. He was very nice in his own way, too. His policing competence rescued me. He had more than a suspicion about what really happened on the canals there. In the end, he too believed in more than he saw. He could imagine things."

"Heaven knows what he'd make of Stourhead."

"You just wonder how in Scotland, England, and Wales, I suppose the whole British Isles and abroad too, the gods managed to have so many temples erected for them—a secret belief in myths and stories in the image of man!—but reminding them of virtues and tragedies—and then how to reconcile this while still engaged in Christian belief!"

Rosalinde smiled mischievously. "So right you are. Stourhead gives one of the finest examples of helping the gods to splendid temples, but what of the village church and Alfred's Tower? What of the River God and his Nymph?"

ABDULLAH

Decked out in unobtrusive clothes with her hair hidden in grey patterned veils, Abdullah was contemplating her new involvements. She knew how wise it was to remain inauspicious. But, on the other hand, she wanted to make a difference.

She had argued with her friends. "I don't show up. I know I don't show up. But I want Muslim family obscurity and at the same time I want to be counted as a woman."

"You love to be simple, don't you! You—no doubt about it—you will crash head-on with yourself!" her friend Alysia replied in exasperation. "Why don't you just accept a rich marriage and quit trying to rip off your veils and rig them on again! Stop being a flashing point! Calm down and stop twitching on gender rights!"

Abdullah was young. She insisted on maintaining a bright future, working towards women's independence, but at the same time fitting into communities. How these goals were to be united remained the dilemma. She was on no account giving up being Muslim or, paradoxically, being a fighter for women's rights.

Sitting as she was on a drystone wall in the countryside, her bubbling, internal turmoil hidden, as havoc is, underneath veils and veils of cultural sedateness, slim and beautiful with hidden but tidy hair, mascara and vivid lipstick, she struck others as promising.

Alysia and others adored her.

Abdullah was looking out over the distant temples, the landscapes and the trees, Britain springing to life after winter bleakness. Her name meant 'Servant of God'. She had been given the name regardless of gender. Her mother had told her early on that this was a compliment. She knew it was a compliment. But at school and everywhere she felt torn. She was both part of the British culture and Muslim practices. She went to a British school and remained Muslim at home.

Her mother was very attractive, even though only

her face was visible under her choice of vivid red, paisley blue and other charming, multi-coloured scarves and veils. Her mother, beautiful, but practical, had admonished her. "Every female knows she quietly reigns. If you remain quiet and unobtrusive, you get your own way. You disregard orders, but you don't loudly object to them, ever. In this way you do your own thing, and no-one's the wiser."

Abdullah thought this fine, if you accepted arranged marriages and doing all the household duties. "But what about all of us with new goals. What about aspiring to be new feisty women, the coming of age of our gender. We were locked up, silenced, when we debated this. What about this day and age, this more acceptable future?"

She was not a person who favoured being silent and especially not a woman who liked swallowing her views. She thought living in Britain was best expressed in what she maintained was the right feminist approach.

She grinned nicely and looked compliant in her long robes and well-hidden, veiled figure. However, she chose why and when she did things. It was not evident to those that noticed her in her very ordinary, grey, Muslim robes. But she had always said to Alysia, "I am very attracted to the English language saying, 'speak softly, but carry a big stick'."

After many struggles, she went her own way—down paths which pleased her own mind.

As she pointed out to her friends, "This is all to the good. I remain Muslim in my dress code and still at the same time I am a feminist." She intended to be outspoken. "I want to join the womanly figures making a mark."

She ducked into anonymity, but held to her views.

Chance brought her into the murky meeting-rooms of a radical right-wing organisation. She was curious about the placards, so she entered a large room. The doors were open. But whatever the organisation was, it certainly, it appeared, did not have the objective of women's equal rights. She had wanted to hear the speaker talk about this.

Oddly enough, next to the seat she had taken on the edge of the audience in this ornate building, sat a bright, seemingly intelligent, effusive, close-cropped, well-shaven man. He was listening intently to the podium speaker, who in turn was advocating serious interventions, particularly when many people were too weak to take up demonstrations of their own or, as the speaker said, did not intervene enough through heckling.

Abdullah had chanced on this meeting. She was herself surprised to be a listener in this mostly right-wing gathering.

But she decided to talk with that well-dressed, quiet and composed man next to her. She wanted some information.

They bonded surprisingly quickly, although in gender and culture they were miles apart. He helped her reconcile living in two cultures as he was very polite. He was self-effacing.

Beneath his sedateness, however, he was assessing her value as an unobtrusive woman since he quickly saw advantage in using such grey ladies as a pawn in his own ploys. He had been sympathetic to the waves and waves of people protesting dictatorships in the Middle East. But losing allegiance to confusing political parties and their many disparate demands, he was now pursuing nothing but his own goals. He no longer cared if one set was fighting for democracy or oligarchy. His aim was to increase his shiny, massive pile in the bank.

He sat in on rallies of the far right. They seemed to him to be less messy, more dedicated to wearing suits, ironed shirts and knowledge of how to invest successfully. He felt unobtrusive there. His good clothes and good looks let him blend in.

He angled his face and fixed the speaker in his gaze. He looked intent. But he was thinking about how he could sell his cache of weapons. Would automatic rifles be enough? They had better be sold along with hand-grenades.

But being suddenly startled by her talking to him, he became abruptly aware of his neighbour. He was sitting on the outer rim of the audience encircling the speaker. There were some empty chairs near him. And a grey-veiled Muslim and very young woman had edged next to him. He politely said hello *sotto voce*.

She didn't stay silent. She said hello too—but she looked at him fiercely.

"I think I've come to the wrong place—perhaps you could help me—and explain in what way that speaker wants our attention and commitment."

He assessed the peculiarity of the situation at once. He had not been to the Middle East for nothing. He knew about chaperones and the difficulties of any Muslim female being anywhere on her own.

"Look, I'll be your alibi. I'll be attentive, and pretend to be servant to your every whim, and deny you've come here or even your speaking to me. I won't trouble you. You can do what you like and I won't bother you. I'll look the other way," and he smiled a contained, non-personal, non-committal smile.

They chatted. She felt safe, and drawn to him. They listened to the podium speaker, an advocate of nationalist values. They spoke to each other, intrigued, and stayed seated as the audience left.

After ascertaining the strong character of the

woman in the chair next to him, James Owen decided she was what he needed: a woman who would be pitied for belonging to a minority, but who had strengths that he wanted. She would fit his purpose.

"But you, in return, must aid my plans," he said. "I am constructing a supply chain to the Middle East. That, in itself, must remain under the radar, very secretive, to all in this region and indeed everywhere else. You know how to appear innocent—you have the clothes for it and you're very self-effacing," he whispered so she could just hear it.

"You mean we should form an alliance of convenience? We should pretend meekness and kindness?" She turned to him.

His face was a mask of male benevolence. "There's nothing like a beneficial liaison," he said.

OWEN AND ABDULLAH were strange partners, each positioned at the opposite end of any scale set up. Owen was in need of her to camouflage his purported interest in charitable causes; she used him for her own ends and because he behaved himself and kept the distance she wanted. In the long run, though, she and he encouraged the ties each had in different ways to the conflicts that raged in the Middle East.

While Owen supplied guns and ammunition to

whoever wanted them, Abdullah desired action that showed how dominant the female gender could be. She would select and motivate only people prepared to share her principles. In this way they were ignorant of each other's character. If Abdullah needed an alibi through male patronage, she had one; on the surface, he needed her in guiding him in current events and regional loyalties.

But there was also a strange mutual attraction neither admitted. Owen was not susceptible to new entanglements. Abdullah wanted nothing more than freedom. But their smiling at each other contravened their separate reasoning selves.

It was a liaison of catastrophic impressions. He thought he directed her every move; she was sure he obeyed her. Stourhead was the place of camouflage which brought them together. It had no internal walls. Its temples and statues were ideal for hiding things. They could be tourists. Strange but ever so ordinary.

IN THE SPREAD EAGLE

Elizabeth was finishing her fish and chips. She was dipping into some last fries with the tartness of ketchup attached.

She watched as other guests arrived. She was pausing and looking up.

There was this portly, but powerful man, very muscular, who didn't seem English, but sported all the right English clothes. He was almost in front of her. He wore an open Burberry car-length coat, a colourful tie, a tweed jacket and polished leather shoes; the latter not very serviceable on gritty paths, she thought.

Strange and not strange. Familiar but not familiar. She had seen him somewhere before, and she searched her memory to find his image.

He darted a look in her direction. Then looked

away again. Abruptly, all at once, he came to a halt. He turned towards her and took a tentative step in her direction.

The coin dropped. In an instant she knew who he was. And she was very surprised. She had departed Germany and he had stayed. She certainly hadn't expected to see him here. But here he was, gazing over at her.

"How extraordinary," she said to herself.

And she added more loudly: "How nice to see you, but so far from home, and are you here for pleasure, or on police business?" She had met him as the Inspector in charge of police investigations in the city of Dessau, Germany. In fact, he had been more than kind to her when they were investigating the use of the Woerlitz landscape garden's watery canals and their illegitimate co-option in the drugs trade. Indeed, she had been rescued by him. But he had maintained a polite distance. So very proper as a police inspector. None-the-less there was a tinge of pleasant, prickling anticipation as he approached.

"I am off duty and a great pleasure it is, to stay in a country with such great pubs; and close to such intriguing sights, such as this English landscape garden. What a small world, as they say.

"I'm on holiday and I've just arrived in this country. I was following the footsteps of Louise von Anhalt-Dessau and her husband in 1775. Among other things, she counted all the steps to the top of Alfred's Tower and enjoyed the view over Wiltshire. I'm interested in seeing how Stourhead was an important model for the Dessau-Woerlitz landscape garden, one of the first to be designed in Germany.

"And Stourhead, this very early landscape garden, was such a strong influence while Henry Hoare was still alive—he died in 1785—only they never met him. Probably when these aristocrats visited he was in London." He stopped momentarily, hopeful there might be a mutual interest.

"I'm glad to have run into you," Inspector Queberon added politely. "At least I can be sure to receive some interesting information. And no doubt I can look forward to trouble coming my way." He chuckled, recalling their last encounter when, after the violent car crash which introduced them, he had later also helped her out of the water. She had nearly drowned near the anchored ferry where a speedboat had been sent to finish them off.

"Nothing will bother you," she laughed, "no trouble brewing in this ancient garden," she smiled in return, "nothing in the line of difficulties like in Woerlitz, excepting you might be interested in why Stourhead is such a magical place. And that will be the only thing I can trouble you with. I'm seeking clarity for myself on several things, and you may get an earful!

"I will make you pay attention despite you wanting to relax! That mix-up that occurs when the Greco-Roman gods and British Liberty meet should occupy your mind, for one thing." And she extended her hand in true German fashion.

He gave her his hand to shake in return.

"There is something, in all politeness, I must ask," Inspector Queberon ventured. "Since it's you, and since you're here, may I join you at your table?" He went on, polite, but happy to not spare her his presence. And he confided what he intended to do.

"I especially want to visit the grotto and look out over the water. The whole garden is built to have a sightline over water. Maybe the River God in Stourhead that I've seen pictured is a signal that the waters should be taken seriously." He crossed his fingers that she might expound on this, a central theme in landscape gardens.

He had wanted a guide, and now, by happy circumstance, and it being a small world, he had exactly what he was looking for. Elizabeth was extremely knowledgeable and would provide him with her interpretation of Stourhead, which was sure to be of an extremely high quality. The gods were kind indeed.

He settled himself at her table without delay. She made no objection; in fact, she was secretly delighted to have him join her. Not that she gave any outward sign of it. She pretended to him that she wanted her interpretation of Stourhead verified. Which was true. She needed an audience, and what better one than an observant police inspector? She would trial her interpretation and see if he was intrigued. She would tell him her thoughts and hope for some positive signals from him.

Elizabeth leaned confidingly close. Dispensing with any preliminary small talk, she began her exhortation. She did not hide her knowledge—or even her teacher-like tone. If he was ready to listen, she would be able to be herself, intrigued, but showing that she was wearing her love of Stourhead lightly.

There seemed no diversion towards flirtatiousness in speaker or listener as they lost track of the world's usual business, excluding all else but the two of them.

"Let us start with the Temple of Flora. Ceres is sometimes mixed up with Flora, but they are mother and daughter in the legends of the goddesses. Both are the female gods of vegetation and plenty. Flora also masquerades as Ceres, the goddess of grain, leaf, and harvest. She has as much influence there as Ceres, her dear mother, has. They both direct the wellbeing of harvests and plants. They are responsible for growth. That's why they are venerated as goddesses.

"Henry Hoare, mark the man, put the Temple of

Flora in front of Neptune rising in the lake with his spume of seahorses. The horn of plenty begins in water. It has a connection with harvests. And you'll notice the river god has no oar, but points upward, and, yes, also outward, to Neptune, who, unfortunately, is no longer there.

"This all has to do with Hercules, who is, after all, the focus of the most dramatic building in Stourhead, the Pantheon. Hercules, leaning on his club and with the lion-skin draped over his shoulder, has, famously, twelve tasks to perform. Whichever way you count them, one, the one that was important to Henry Hoare, was to decide whether Hercules would choose an upward, rocky path of virtue or the soft, easy life. So immediately behind him a rocky path leads upwards.

"Then there was Hercules' entanglement with the spirit of Meleager, he who was in the last analysis responsible for his fight with a river god. That was when Hercules broke the river god's horn of plenty."

The Inspector was more than indulgent and Elizabeth was enthralled herself: "The gods of water are an obvious pairing, even though ocean and river are distinct in their manifestations."

She bent forward, forgetting dessert. His eyes were shining towards her, his lips were parted. He was oblivious to anything around him.

Elizabeth became the advocate of mythic waters. She believed in their incarnations in statues and in their many symbols and wanted the Inspector to suspend the cynicism of all his police-force years. She was being a Naiad herself.

She went on, "Neptune strengthens the might of the river's source, as all rivers flow to the sea. Neptune often occurs in gardens. In Wilhelmshoehe, in southern Germany, with which you might be familiar," and here she smiled again at the Inspector, "Neptune's presence is evoked where the cascade from the mount of Hercules ends in the lake construed for the god of water and oceans.

"Neptune sits there in Wilhelmshoehe with his trident under the flowing waters that spill over its last basin. His minions the Tritons blow loudly from their conch shells as the water runs down to burst upwards again in a high arc from the mouth of a rock. This rock has the face of a giant, recalling the story of how Hercules defeated the giants. This is recalled in the waters spuming in the landscape garden in Wilhelmshoehe in the German city of Kassel. And it is a theme resplendent again in the presentation of the powers of mythological beings in Stourhead as well. They celebrate the same power of water in Stourhead.

"Giants," she continued, after a glance to make sure he was still spell-bound, "are the personification of the subterranean embedded in the earth's interior, its inner force. As the Tritons repeat the waters' roar, the earth's elemental force is turned into a garden. The waters rise into a formal pool in Wilhelmshoehe and flow down once more into the largest basin containing the cascade, the basin presided over by the god hidden behind the downward rush of its falling waters, Neptune."

The Inspector heard her out. He liked his police knowledge augmented by her deep scouring of relevant sources, and, to tell the truth, he liked her passionate immersion—so distant from his surface scepticism. Her eyes glowed. Her face reflected how concentrated her whole being was. She was giving him more than dry knowledge. She was imparting her feeling of why these sea gods were of consequence.

He watched as the dusk set in and the candles were lit to glow on the tables. Elizabeth had created a world and he was imagining it in his mind. He had let go any intrusive clattering and entered where she pointed out his emotion and attention should be. He was glad to forget all else and was turning the meaning of water over in his mind. More than that common stuff that was mostly cold and wet, he saw that it was commanded by the harsh god of the waves and could lead to the kingdom below the earth. He had now to consider

Stourhead as more than just going on an ornamental walk.

Water drew the celestial and the earthly together into one elemental whole, both higher and lower reaches flowing into one another. He contemplated the elemental in landscape gardens. How water and earth intertwined as a spiritual statement. This made them transcend each element. It opened them both to an interpretation beyond each separate science. And the twain shall meet he reasoned, looking into her eyes.

And she went on.

"Earthly existence relies on water being the door, opaque but enchanting, that links the upper world to the lower one."

Aware of this at last, and listening to Elizabeth, the Inspector not only appreciated anew what Stourhead offered him, but was ready to accept activity beyond the material world. He opened his mind to an otherworldly universe.

He was not above believing that the strange manifestation of the river gods was serious. He thought that here were the fates intervening. Fortuitously, too, they had brought him and Elizabeth together.

ON GOING TO BED

Elizabeth cast an eye over her room.
She was proud of herself for not having wavered in her lengthy explanation over the dinner table. She joked to herself that Queberon, too, had not—even ever so politely—walked away.

Stourhead was dear to her. But now alone in this her room she was unsure of herself and her chance meeting with Queberon. The evening had been exhilarating. At least explaining in detail about the landscape garden had not been in vain. It was objective enough. She was finding the right words.

Her bed was made up and its neatness invited rest. She was determined to disturb its white sheets and red silk coverings. But first she must take her pearl necklace off and her earrings. She sat down at the dressing table and looked in the mirror directly in front of her.

Her black frizzy hair framed her face. It reached out in curly spirals, partly covering her brow and the sides of her pale skin. She saw her deep, dark eyes. They seemed to elongate at the corners and dwarf her smallish nose.

She admitted she was tired at the end of the day and unsure of how much of her wrinkles were hidden—her voice quavered, then her face showed a quivering smile and she no longer sat straight. Her back slumped into a question mark.

It turned rigid in the next seconds. Behind her appeared Mrs. Grimm. But—yes—Elizabeth was certain she had locked the door, ascended the stairs by herself and she was quite sure she was alone in the room.

There in the mirror was the face of the charming old lady. She was smiling with good grace at Elizabeth. And she fixed her with an amber glint in her very attentive eyes. Her unwavering glance made the room darken.

"To be sure, you are embarking on the right journey. I welcome you here. You are needed in Stourhead." Mrs. Grimm flashed her tight knuckles and veined, translucent blue hands. She waved them in an arc as if gathering in a vast audience dedicated to her, watchful and within grasp.

Elizabeth sat frozen. She dared not move.

Mrs. Grimm kept to the mirror as if she owned it.

She spoke, "You must put things right. There are forces in your beloved Stourhead which are boding no good. You are obliged to the River God. You see things others don't. Trust in the immaterial and the gods. They have strength and are present here, ever listening and watchful, especially if their temples are used for illegitimate purposes."

She turned her back and the darkness of the mirror seemed to have endless rooms into which she strode. Her lithe figure, belying her age, shone like a burning light. The light gleamed steadily and then she was gone.

Elizabeth was shaken to the core. But she revived, although she felt haunted. She was surrounded by the old lady's familiar scent. It captured her, and enveloped her, smoothing her neck and shoulders. They had been so tense. Her hands, too, became soft, and she flexed them, becoming aware of a new youthfulness and purpose.

She lit a lamp by her bedside.

THE INSPECTOR WAS TIRED. He had learned a great deal and he was grateful for it. He was intent on retaining it—so he was saying things to himself over and over again in order to commit the most important things to his memory. It was like a mantra and in the middle, somewhere, he fell asleep. He was a white shape covered with blankets and deeply surrounded with pillows almost covering his face.

And he dreamed. He was in a fine landscape and he was a Herculean figure. But entering this infinity, muscular and attentive, he saw nothing but blackness, even seeing no reflection. Nothing but noncommittal space. He had to move forward.

Out of the blackness, Elizabeth took his arm. First his fingers and then his elbow became visible where she was, in the mirror. She was helping him to regain consciousness. He was in and out of his dream.

He saw his reflection gaining shape. He bent his dreaming mind to the coordination of his muscles and displaying a focussed self. He was seeking his becoming whole. He extended himself. He recognized himself and did not.

He was dreaming he would find his true self. There in the mirror. And this would reflect back. He struggled. He strained. He wanted his image to leave the cave of darkness that had always been his. His cave of darkness where he had always simply followed procedure. He hid under the duvet, caught in the pillows.

And then he flailed and cast coverings and pillows and all aside.

He woke.

He could not see himself in the mirror. It was too dark.

But his future was circling the room like a phantom. It was about how he would commit himself. He had always been a top-notch detective and very conscientious. But what about his unconscious feelings? He had remained aloof in his own private life. He had never opened the door to love and those roller-coaster upheavals of the emotions this brought.

He had muscles and a honed body; he was physically strong, but his desires were dulled, kept closed.

The light grew in the early dawn as he tossed and turned. Standing, he stumbled to the window to take a deep breath. He could see indistinct outlines. The whole landscape garden was mysterious. The lake and the cascades of the Stour stood out, luminous and silvery. The woods were dark and he thought the black branches were stretching. Their buds were fists uncurling as they brandished their first delicate green leaves clenched in dark leather gloves. Liveliness was stealing in, unfolding, reaching out in the coming dawn light. And he became aware of his needs. Night-thoughts reigned.

He had not plumbed the landscape garden's depths yet; had not yet turned his life around.

IN THE INSPECTOR'S MIND

Sitting as the sun came up on the grass before the Palladian Bridge, viewing how shadow and light intertwined, Inspector Queberon was intrigued to see before him such an early manifestation of a thought-out landscape garden. He imbibed his peaceful surroundings. He had come from abroad for precisely this reason: to sit and let peace envelop him. He was glad to let his eyes travel the sumptuous panorama of lake and Pantheon. The trees were majestic, hanging mint green in arched boughs and framing the stone buildings.

The Inspector gazed raptly at the Stourhead Pantheon. It was the home of the Greek gods and Henry Hoare had placed it in the middle of the valley the river incised in the landscape. The Inspector imagined Hercules in the niche in the Pantheon and at the centre of all the gods. Hercules had a toned and muscular body, not unlike his own. The Inspector had trained his body every day on his German bicycle. And Hercules reigned with his club laid carefully next to the lion skin he was wearing, alluding to his muscular might which he had brought to bear in his twelve labours.

The Inspector's leisure hours, such as they were, divided nicely between his reading habits and his bicycle. He had been told by the so focussed Elizabeth about Hercules, the semi-god who was so important in the early landscape gardens.

In the 1700s these assembled gods still personified virtues, traits smothered in the present century. In the past many visited the temples to the gods. Hercules, he had been told, was not known in the centuries which had passed for his powerful masculinity alone, but renowned for his restraint. He had a perfect body, yes, but he made you think of trying the path that was hardest, that of turning away lust, dissipation, and anger. The perfect body was aligned to the perfect mind.

Hercules had tussled with a river god. He had broken off a horn as the river god turned himself into a steer, but the river god and Hercules had both venerated and left intact the horn of plenty.

Legends were ripe, and Horatio Queberon sat in the morning sun meditating and glad he was away from his duties. He contemplated how right it was to have a model. His thoughts were all on Hercules.

Hercules was the great mediator. Jupiter, among others, wanted him to accomplish impossible tasks; Hercules completed them, and seemed more than human. He was human and also divine in what he did, recalled Horatio Queberon. Hercules was singly admired for straightforwardly rectifying things that had markedly gone awry.

Hercules was model to all who wanted justice and good, and the impossible to be put right. He was also the human/divine one who chose the steep, rocky path of virtue over the luxurious life of plenty. Henry Hoare must have thought the same when he chose Hercules for his Pantheon.

What the Inspector was not noticing, was the solid Englishness of the model village near which he was sitting on his grassy knoll. Indeed he was staring at the Otherworldliness of the gods in the form of their residence in the Pantheon. But around him were the village church and the medieval spire of the Bristol Cross. The scene was tranquil. But it showed tiers and tiers of mythical waypoints ascending the Stour valley.

In the great distance was Alfred's Tower, with its inscription of the king who defended and instigated Britain's Liberty. It was far away from the Inspector's eye, but there to be seen nonetheless.

In fact it was straight in front of him, a beeline from the nest of church spire, and the inn, surrounding him where he sat. But the Inspector was still entranced by the sunrise and by his thoughts on Hercules.

The sunlight glowed first from the top of the valley, shortly afterwards sending its rays downward. Sparkling, the beams came from the east. Slowly the Pantheon glowed in the light.

It was a heavenly valley.

When all was doused in sunlight, Inspector Queberon noticed Elizabeth striding, and slipping, on the wet grass towards him. She wore such serviceable clothes, he was sure she was about to go sleuthing in the gardens.

She surprised him however as she sat down next to him on his stretched-out coat. She looked him in the eye and gloried in the setting. They engaged in small talk, but in the end, she regaled him once more with knowledge he was certain to need, engaged as he was now in studying Stourhead, and prepared to spend quite a few of his days here. She was as abrupt and decisive as ever. Prickly, he thought, and smiling deeply to himself he called it that.

"Greek orders must be learnt, as anyone not an architect must learn where ornamentation comes from and what it means. Certainly the knowledge of the gods and their myths is not imbibed with normal Sunday school teaching," she said, and added: "So that too is a world entered into and invited into the mind while engaging with new languages, Latin and Greek, and with their fabled literature. Henry Hoare the Magnificent remarked that reading entranced him, letting him relinquish gazing out of his window!"

She was at this moment, and in the sunlight, unstoppable.

"Arcadia was an ideal. Its realisation was a work of pleasure. In it the love of nature, particularly trees, and the celebration of nature's gods, Ceres, Flora, and the nymphs, are personified. All the gods and goddesses in the Parthenon are paramount. You find, my dear Inspector, everything sacred in this special valley before us. It comes together here."

She turned to him, wishing profoundly he were as avid in taking this valley to heart as she was.

"Myths are readings and celebrations of nature, whether antique or contemporary, a means of gaining access to pictures in the mind.

"Both the Greek revival, its republicanism, and the Picturesque are means of re-imagining the world in which we live. They superimpose alternatives. We begin to think differently."

Elizabeth was convinced Henry Hoare had created a garden that exemplified the Greek gods and their legends. It was not just academic to come and see what he had done. She embraced it. She went on: "The picturesque and the landscape gardens have a very sociable quality. Not only are they the result of planning, but also of the connection between people, between father and child or husband and wife, or friendships."

Elizabeth was looking straight at him. He was considering—at the very first level—friendship, not constrained now by duties to the Dessau police, but free. Inspector Queberon was none-the-less flustered. He was all right within institutional bounds. Freedom was another thing entirely.

Elizabeth went on.

"It takes a wealth of knowledge to unlock the multiple meanings alluded to, of necessity, only silently. Statues, temples and parks can only show myths; we are needed to bring them to life. As the stories awaken, and we come to know them, so does the sacred landscape."

He was not sure he could make up each relevant story, seeing her use so much varied insight. She was, of course, pointing him in the right direction. Perhaps, on the other hand, he was creative enough to combine or envision his own story and attach it to one of the stories told of the gods. Perhaps he could elevate his good fortune to tell the tale of a god so strong as he believed would count as a convincing attribute of his own. The myths merged with one's choice as to the future. The silent words of the Pantheon were there to increase choosing and potency. Henry Hoare had done the same. He had selected the gods he believed in.

Elizabeth turned anew to him, a wondrous glow in her eyes. "Water is the fluid centre that unites the Underworld and the realm of light, the sacred entry to enchanted ground.

"Come with me now, this minute. I'm going to explore the heart of the matter, that is, the grotto, where the Nymph in her cave and the River God reside. They sit level with the water. All the other gods are in their heights. You and I will appreciate the rocky look-out between the Nymph and the River God. It frames by its sightline the very knoll you're sitting on. And, it frames, too, the medieval and gothic village and its Englishness you care so much about. It is joined in its old Englishness with republican values. That is what the Greek city-state and Roman Republicanism show, when you visually combine them, in the long sightline up from the village bridge to the Pantheon."

She got up. He consented. He was giving her the latitude of his holiday mood, but it was a study in having to be convinced. Wherever one looked in the forest there was this glimmer. There was this glow. The eye picked up the fish-like bodies of the many leaves. They floated in circles in a school of scales and reflected light. The forest was an ocean. The waves were green and then darkened to a network. He was emotionally the same as the leaves either brown from last year or dancing in the wind or just appearing in new spring mint green. Last year's leaves were forming a base and circling in a waltz wherever a gust of wind animated them. They seemed to be talking.

Elizabeth longed for him to pay attention to this moment and preserve it, for the simple sake of his forever knowing what Stourhead meant. And it meant to her so much more than just gazing out at its beauties. She was adamant that the landscape, designed as it was, could touch his inner soul.

It was the reason she had come. She was willing the Inspector not only to take in the surroundings, but their careful calibration, the thought-out setting.

She went on by saying: "The lake in Stourhead is not just a visual asset, but adds the depth of storytelling. It refers to the sanctuary of Diana and her epiphany in woodland and by the water, a place where the goddess dwells. And it refers to Virgil and the search for his fulfilment. It has so many meanings, but they are precise ones. Not superficial by any means. The lake seen from the grotto locates the places where the gods reside and are worshipped."

The lake, as Elizabeth knew, sat very low with steep ridges above on all sides. They were forested, with the lakeside path leading in and out of plantings of broad-leaf trees and evergreens. The predominance of water and dense trees reminded all in the know of the classical sites of Lake Nemi and Lake Avernus. These were the places, given to the goddesses here in Stourhead again, where below the waters and above, transit was possible. The goddesses were not confined to the world above or below.

She impressed on the Inspector that paintings as visual compositions and landscape were seen as a whole. She was adamant about this and turned pleadingly toward him.

"The topographical and romantic drawings and paintings of the eighteenth century made these views easily recognisable. So many relevant ones are kept in the rooms of the mansion house. Even the one where Hercules decides whether to choose the life of easy dissipation or that of the rock-strewn path of virtue is kept there.

"Colt-Hoare, the man who was Henry Hoare's successor, went to Italy, to Rome and Naples, and he interested J. W. Turner in the Sibyl's enticing Virgil into the Underworld at Lake Avernus. Because of its close visual affinity with these sites, Stourhead follows the template of the lake in the sacred grove. It seems to me that these people treasured the divine world. The creator of Stourhead loved the strength Hercules showed and the inheritor admired the advice given by the Sibyl to Aeneas to come to the Otherworld to learn from his father.

"The stillness is so untroubled that nature is perfectly mirrored in the water. Water is the gateway to the Otherworld of the gods."

Elizabeth stopped. She was at a standstill. She had reached the point she wanted to impress him with most of all. She needed him to acknowledge that water, or the water of life, was the symbolic road taken after death. She meant the journey from upper to lower world with which all the ancients were familiar.

She was uncertain that the Inspector would still pay attention. She was giving him the benefit of her vast knowledge, but when would he tire of it? He was unceasingly polite. Part of it was professional habit, but she was now beyond that in giving him her interpretation. Was he willing to enter this world of immersion in so many things that only made sense when seen together, one intensifying the other?

The lake was so still that no breeze rippled its waters. The Inspector raised his eyes in a penetrating gaze to Elizabeth's own brown ones. "This," he said falteringly, then decisively, "was called the mirror of Diana, twin sister of Apollo and protectoress of woodland and water? Her companions are nymphs. Avernus, associated with the Sibyl, is the lake near the Cumaen sanctuary and is also a gateway to the Otherworld."

He was learning minutely what she said, but also delving into his memory, what he had read in his books. This was unfamiliar territory, but he was slowly becoming enthused. He was following her. She took advantage, and pressed her observation to its limit.

"The theme of the Underworld is represented by the grotto placed at eye-level on the lake. The grotto looks to the lake, the place of mirroring. But the downward look to the depths of the Underworld is enthralled through its eye to heights connecting it to illumination, as it looks up to the Temple of Apollo. A pathway of meaning is created with this sightline, the passage from dark to light and from Underworld to the heavens, as a journey of death and renewal."

Elizabeth drew a large breath. She was not sure that the Inspector was listening to her emphasis on minute detail. But she was sure of what she was saying and wanted very much for him to know all that she was thinking.

He moved his legs in their leather boots, but only to sink more deeply into the grass. He was actually glad she was sharing her knowledge. Inspector Queberon was not of the type that condemned women for knowing what mattered.

She was so enthusiastic, she drew him forward, blissfully happy that here was a man very much interested in listening to her.

She ventured to ask him to accompany her into more of this beautiful valley and domain of the gods.

IN ELIZABETH'S EYES

For once it would be agreeable to be second in command.

Elizabeth's eyes delved into Queberon's, as she gestured vividly with her hand towards the rocky outcrop, dusky and stony, but clearly at the water's edge, which represented the middle of the grotto. They were now both opposite it on the lake. They had the 'eye' of the rock in full view, where the River God was pointing upwards.

"Under the grotto's cupola and rough stone arches," she said, "the statues of the nymph and the River God are surprising with their white marble presence. One, you will find, is in repose and the other faces towards us directly.

"The element of water is related to our reflections, be they grief or healing—either to wash, or dip in water is a sacred action, and always has been, dear Inspector. And it is wise to continue a sacred mission because the River God is giving Aeneas instruction in his despair. The river gives him advice to ascend to enlightenment.

"Water, you'd think it negligible, but here it produces the movement which helps convey us from darkness to light. Or, if you will, it connects the mere springs of the Stour to sublime understanding. The direction the path takes towards the Pantheon and, ultimately to the Temple of Apollo, tells you as much."

They were walking now opposite the River God's opening onto the lake. The trees were in their first unfolding mode, green and pristine in their lovely freshness. The Temple of Apollo reigned above them, across the lake and very high up, now smothered in reddish-pink rhododendrons. These were new, relatively speaking, as they had not graced this high temple of the god in the mid-eighteenth century.

Elizabeth tended to discount the frippery of rhododendrons and their candy colour beauty.

"The view of the 'eye' to the upper world includes the village and temples in the garden. In this encounter with the nature god, he finally frees the ascent: the pathway leads upwards.

"In the Pantheon you will find Hercules and

other deities. Then there is another wealth of meaning added to the others. Heliopolis is where the sun god Apollo reigns. He is the opposite of darkness and Underworld."

Inspector Queberon could not but marvel. He could not but pay homage. Elizabeth was using light and dark as if all humanity, no matter the century it was in, paid attention to the universal truth attached to this landscape design.

The Underworld encompassed what he professionally encountered, but in so different a form. Were all those goons and bashers, those criminals and liars, from the Underworld? Or are we all at the mercy of devils?

They were rounding the lake, where the Chinese Bridge used to be, a white bridge not unlike the one in the Luisium in Dessau. The Inspector was learning more than he thought through a voice that was reverent, a voice that began to be like music to his ears.

"Pre-Christian civilisations honoured each lake and river through its presiding deity," she went on, testing him on his knowledge of the ancient ways.

"The water spirit was a spirit of place. Pagan shrines often arose where important water deities resided, in particular where Roman religion incorporated places that had been sacred previous to them.

"Water was associated with purification and healing. Such powers were linked to the sun setting and rising. The qualities of the sun, as giver of life and light, were invested in water because the sun set and rose in bodies of water. The god of the sun was seen as uniting with the water deity in the marriage of opposite principles."

Elizabeth linked this with the Celts. She said these Ancients were scattered throughout Germany, too. She looked enticingly at him.

"And where the sun set, the dead entered everlasting life. That was why the West and the sunset on the endless Western ocean were so sacred. Principles that endure when we look and forever honour our passing days but mighty involvement with the colourful elements of water and air."

Not so different from the two of us, thought the Inspector to himself. She, in her red coat gleaming below every tree—and me in this serviceable Burberry, attentive; we could be seen as true opposites, like water and air, elements which cannot exist one without the other, getting closer, involved with one another? She is emphasizing and telling me the most arcane, but pertinent, wisdom associated with the first English landscape gardens. Opposites attract. Do I believe this: opposites attract!

With her Celtic gravity, Elizabeth expounded some more on the water and its meaning.

"Water is related to the Underworld and makes darkness turning to light and light returning to darkness real. This cyclical archetype has water and the Underworld partaking of the rites of passage. The shrines to water and its healing powers are to be found throughout Europe, often being a happy marriage of earlier deities of place and Roman gods and goddesses."

Elizabeth and the Inspector were nearly at the grotto.

"Thus at Badenweiler a Celtic holy well was dedicated to Diana Abnoba, the goddess of the Black Forest, and at Buxton the hot springs were dedicated to the goddess of the grove, while at Bath the powers of its healing waters were aligned with the goddess Minerva. In this way many people honoured the gods which were spirits of place. The gods helped in need and they were invoked."

She wanted the Inspector to find it in him to reach the same conclusion that she did. In the last analysis, she had entrusted to him her deep musings. And this as someone she had only now realized was trustworthy and perhaps as much in love as she was with this unique habitat of sacred wood and sacred valley. She turned to him and said: "The reverence for water was incorporated in nearly all of the important Graeco-Roman Deities. And where it was, it added another layer of meaning. This was extended to include associations in Diana's wood or the places that were the haunt of the muses."

They had arrived. Elizabeth drew fresh breath. Inspector Queberon gazed, marvelling at her. There had been a sea-change. Only he, as he thought, was as yet aware of it.

Elizabeth was adding some last comments, although in her case they sounded like beliefs. She particularly liked attributing Diana with her special role as the goddess of the forest and the hunt.

"The grotto is where the river god and the nymph reign. It is linked by its 'hanging woods' to the sanctuary of Diana of the Sacred Grove. The powers of water to heal and purify, venerated in the pagan sanctuaries, become imbued with qualities akin to human emotion."

And finally, they were in the grotto. She looked directly at Queberon. She began to wish for more of his company.

"This quality of veneration is added because of the association with Egeria, one of the nymphs accompanying Diana. Alexander Pope revered her in his grotto and wrote the words engraved before her statue in the Stourhead grotto." She finished this insight, but immediately went on.

"The story of Egeria exemplifies human attachment, in her grief for her husband King Numa. Egeria wept so unceasingly that Diana transformed her tears to a spring. This story turns deep sadness to renewal, exemplified by the resurgence of water in a pure spring rising from deep within the earth. Grief and regeneration are thus part of the meaning of the grotto."

Elizabeth had combined two stories. But each was meaningful. The nymph and Egeria both were elegant as presences for the source of the Stour; better yet, she told the stories in relation to Henry Hoare, who sorrowed over the death of his daughter, but whose garden survived his death and remained, with its lake formed from the Stour River, to be admired by the multitudes who came after him.

Inspector Queberon looked outwards from the rocky chamber and towards the left of its magnificent eye and gazed out at the green and wonderful world. Indeed, all the minute glory of the then and now enhanced the rural parish that had been there in view. But also to be seen were the Temple of Flora and the Temple of Apollo.

Inspector Queberon was trying to add all these things together, as he was wont to do in his detective work. All these elements on the one hand represented what was erected in centuries past and kept engrained throughout history. But the temples to the gods also exerted influence. They kept alive a diverse and incalculable, invisible, action. They didn't adhere to time. The gods appeared and disappeared. They were active in the present and 'time out of time'. They were the unseen in the happenstance of every unplanned event in life and responded to need. It was the influence of the unknown. It was a crossroads.

There were different routes. The rural walk could be taken and tribute to history be paid. But the invocation of the gods was undefined in its consequences—and always a risk, a chance lived now. An individual story could be forevermore lifted to the plane of mythical but true intervention. This was deeply felt by each person, real in its emotion, joy as well as grief, and the gods were responsible. And the gods were the spiritual involvement called in, whether virtuous or mythical, to inspire humans. It was the prototype of what each human in the presence of the gods was meant to feel, in clock time or in the truth of story time. No one was alone in mapping out what was to be or who was there to love.

Inspector Queberon admitted this. And in doing so, he was seeing within his soul and that for the first time. He looked profoundly and deeply at himself.

What he was prepared to recognize in his inner scrutinizing was that Elizabeth was now essential to his life. But would she admit the same? His inner self needed augmentation. He no longer saw himself as complete.

They could not see the Pantheon now. They were climbing the ascent to the Temple of Apollo.

THE TEMPLE OF APOLLO

The highest climb in all of Stourhead went immediately upwards from the Palladian Bridge. The path led them closer but not through the grotto, and it was nearer to the inn. From the vantage point of Apollo's Temple, as Elizabeth pointed out, they could see the whole garden.

They were climbing near the cascades. Then they would triumphantly mount the temple heights. The rushing sound of water added romance in its joyful and uncontrolled bursts and its endless playful resolves. The water gloried in pleasurable uncertainty, as if it knew how entangled those looking at its shining surface might become.

In landscape terms, it reminded of the many tumbling waters rushing down near classical sights. Tivoli and its cascades had been a romantic spur to so many on the Grand Tour in Italy long ago and even now the sound of water, careless and joyful, provided the undertow of sweetness and expectation intrinsic to each and every person enamoured of one another.

Apollo and his temple mirrored the one in Balbec, in Palmyra, so graceful and mindful of the sun god. It was copied in the valley of the Stour and placed to give a view of all below from its placement on the heights. Men and women could sit in the niches and survey the ornamentation of the whole valley. Elizabeth and Queberon stood, entranced, and looked together over the scenes spread out before them.

They surveyed the peaceful valley, the lake and the path rounding it, this other way through the Hanging Wood than the one they had taken this time; all these paths could lead to and reach this wonderful temple. What neither one of them knew was that these paths had been much in use for nefarious purposes.

Elizabeth and Queberon were thankful to see the design and planning that was visible from these heights and how clever Hoare had been to place Apollo's Temple to gently dominate this valley's graceful outlay. The nearby cascades provided the same roaring and tinkling over rocks that Hoare's friend Shenstone had planned in honour of Virgil in his landscape garden, The Leastowes, in the bench near falling water, a bench to sit down upon and to contemplate.

Unknown to them was the disguising note these watery sounds provided for footsteps so contrary to peace and contemplation; paths used for the purpose of trafficking and hiding ill-gotten goods.

Eizabeth was telling Queberon that Henry Hoare had read the Scots adventure story of the findings in Balbec. Robert Wood and James Dawkins had in the year 1757 published their illustrations in the folio book of this abandoned city and its worship of Apollo. They had travelled in then unknown territory to scout Middle Eastern lands, especially to establish true remains of the temples to the gods. Wood and Dawkins adopted the clothes of the Arabs and took natives as guides and went over dunes and deserts to establish monuments and ancient cities in the Orient. "Their portraits, in a pleased agitation amidst camels and native Arabs can be seen," whispered Elizabeth, "in Edinburgh in the National Gallery."

The book that Woods and Dawkins compiled was published and bought by Hoare, and the temple to Apollo in Stourhead was erected the same year. But this was not in the desert, rather on the high ground overlooking all in the Stour landscape garden. Only the terrace next to the house and its sun-symbol atop an obelisk were superior to the pagan symbols. The sun god met his match in the glinting disc perched so neatly on that symbol of resurrection, the obelisk. These explanations received all Elizabeth's and Queberon's attention; they did not in the least think anything would distract them.

Elizabeth was in her element and was saying to the Inspector, "In the sightlines created, the one leading from water to the light of the sun is still basic. It is supported by a layering of references in statues, temples and ornaments.

"If you return to the grotto and the association of River God and nymph, you are reminded of the Tempe, the Arcadian lands of peace and natural beauty associated with that very peaceful valley. It is described by Aeolian, the Greek poet, in terms of idyllic peace."

She dearly wanted him to partake; to become genuinely involved, not only with her learning, but —and she was contemplating something very new —with her. She felt he could engage with her, not just as the second sex providing information—so easily given by her—and not superficially. For the first time she wanted more than sincere attention. She wanted him for herself.

"This valley of Tempe is related to the oceanic god Neptune by a sightline to the ornamental statue of him rising from the waves, sadly no longer in existence here in Stourhead. But the gods of water are an obvious pairing, even though ocean and river are distinct from one another."

She was hopeful. He hadn't moved and was attentive. She tried her last, long sentences on him. She said: "The power of recollection is heightened. It becomes, as in the historical paintings so beloved in this period, an idealised memory. It is connection to an emotional desire: to revere and adore natural beauty not our own."

Elizabeth strongly advocated this concept of painting heightening powers that were within, bringing out in a person's psyche the capacity to see, but to see more in contemplation than in hurried, and brief, acknowledgement.

Her thoughts moved to the champions of material things, the James Owens of this world.

"You know," she said to the Inspector, "there are people who argue that the less emotion, the better. I disagree, wondering if that isn't suppression. When you come to this valley, seeing it from Apollo's Temple, don't you also enter the outlook of the god, at once sublime, and wonderful and yet human when it comes to him being enchanted, all of a sudden, with, for example, the River God Peneos' daughter Daphne. Are you not taken by the spirit of place?

"Are you not agreeing, by the very fact of seeing

this valley, to the place of these gods, to their view of fate and chance; to their lifting of nature into art?"

They were scarcely aware of movement behind them. Someone swift of foot eased from behind a pillar of the temple and quickly charged up the path. She held a bundle swathed in a foreign looking carpet. She stroked it like a baby and she held it carefully as she strode away without a backward glance. Elizabeth caught a glimpse, found the movement strange.

A tingle in her spine reminded her of her unhappy premonitions. She was reminded of the many sounds that had ricocheted from the rustic stones near the River God Thames in Somerset House. This is what they meant. Yet it was a vision not certainty.

The grey-clothed lady was not sprinting, but close to it. Wrapped in her unassuming clothes, she found what she wanted, the pathway that took her into woods. She abruptly hid the article she was carrying beneath her wide sweeping cloak.

The Inspector looked around, wary of such fast movement, his police training coming to the fore. But at that very moment, the financial expert, James Owen, appeared, solid and black-tied, taking in the scene, and focussing their attention. He was almost by the temple, coming up the path.

Elizabeth felt his presence dogging hers. She

could not shake Rosalinde's opinion that no good would come from him. And that he was associated with the grey-clothed woman that had just disappeared so rapidly.

"Well, well," he said. "I run into you at last."

Horatio was watching suspiciously. Could someone, and he eyed Owen, be taking advantage of the temples and statues of the gods and goddesses that are placed in this valley? Surely this Temple of Apollo pointed to only a place where the god held sway?

He observed the stranger carefully.

Keeping his eyes on Elizabeth, James Owen murmured loud enough to be heard: "Looking around, I'd wonder at this neo-classical temple. The original one doesn't need to be imitated! Maybe in pictures, you can construct these edifices, maybe in this light. You might get carried away by the picture, but notice right here, the scalloped edges are way too eccentric; they embellish too much. It becomes frippery, like icing on cakes."

What caught the Inspector's attention was the discrepancy between what Owen was saying with such studied conviction, and his darting glances to take in how his views were provoking Elizabeth.

James Owen was alert and attuned and not at all as nonchalant as he made himself out to be. He knew the Temple of Apollo well. He had come to the temple far too easily and rapidly along the high road.

Indeed, and this became very evident to Queberon, he was now also interested in canvassing every part of the temple as he searched it for someone else. That someone else was known to him, but mysterious—at least from the way he darted looks at each tree, each curve of the rich sandstone, besides his keeping such a watchful eye on the two he had encountered here.

Owen continued to provoke. "Pictures of storms may try to elicit wild feelings of terror and wonder but pictures stay the same thing over and over. Lightning close above the hanging woods and the deep ravine may signal terror and shudders, but look again, and the picture never changes. For about three hundred years, there has been that temple and this valley and the lightning to boot.

"If you were out and caught by thunderstorms, you'd be drenched, and the sodden wetness would overwhelm all the sublime emotion you could possibly feel. And that would be that."

Elizabeth smiled testily. "But the artist shows the ravine and the rocks and pinpoints exactly how terrorizing it can be. No way out. It is up to the viewer to learn, to acknowledge within, what he faces. To remind the lover of landscapes to see the sublime terror and the wonderful, mighty, threat of nature, that's what it's about. To be drenched physically is not the key to it at all but, instead, it is the emotional acknowledgement that matters, an envisioning, the terror of wind and storm that enters body and soul. Nature really lets art be its soul.

"Nowhere is this more strongly expressed than in a landscape like this one before you, the buildings classical, the trees lit and then sombrely dark and wooded. It is the framework for the disappearing and reappearing of the gods."

"Ah," said Owen coolly. "Think of a surgeon at work, where the nurses drape the body in green plastic. All I look at is the hole. I stay rational. I can grasp the need, but never will I be caught in tears at anyone's pain."

Elizabeth stared at him with her dark brown eyes. "The emotion of terror and the sublime was created by the Romantics in order to remind people that no matter the goods and the money, they are human. Your clients, sir, are not just the sterling you gain in transactions. Humans are not quivering jellies of skin, but conscious and capable of reaction and ridden with emotion.

"The landscapes of centuries ago tell a tale of the mythic, the mythopoetic. They are nubile with strange beings, gods that are human in their passions; men and women that are godlike in their despair."

Owen patted the strikingly luminous walls of Apollo's Temple, sliding his hand along the stones.

The Inspector could not but believe that Owen was secretly sending a message, tapping in code. He knew a criminal when he saw one.

TOGETHER, YET APART

Just now, Syria was the name of the game. But it was not the only war that Owen had in mind. With its long and fractious wars, the Middle East provided opportunities of an extraordinary nature.

James Owen was well known in the trade and did not have to look far for suppliers.

Lesser beings would have had lesser aims. Owen turned a blind eye to any suffering civilized communities lobbied against. He only provided "instruments of righteous violence," and looked away—counting, always, on a rich return.

Abdullah, on the other hand, fully believed in the ancient claims made for the fighting strength of her country in the Middle East. Her ode to joy was in the Temple of Apollo modelled on the one now in Syria, in Balbec. This cemented for her the two-way street between the relatively recent democracy of the West and the ancient ways of her own culture. As she was a veiled woman she was not expected to act decisively or independently, but only unobtrusively. And she had selected Owen as her partner. He was not interested in specific causes; he only cared in trading weapons for his own wealth. But that meant she could advise him; he depended on the fact that she, more than he, knew what each faction wanted. She knew the Middle East, he did not. He, not she, cared about money and she, being more aware of the terrain, told him where to sell.

So it was she who had selected Owen. He seemed willing and able, as the English would put it, to risk his life for gain. His profit would be his wealth; hers would be a successful revolution.

She wanted the outward deception of submission as a female that was part of the old Middle East culture, but what she was also learning was to be radical in her own way, as an ever more independent female, emerging slowly and shaking all dependence off. She would glide about pretending she was satisfied as a humble unassuming grey-clothed woman, but she was looking for a life of completion on her own, away from men. And with Owen's dealings, she had influence. She was now going to belong to no culture whatsoever. She was helping

Owen, but perhaps the revolution might be hers in the future. In that case, she would in the end decide who got what.

She wanted to have enough to live on, and she wanted above all to be mistress of her own fate. She was strong within, but looked pliable and accommodating from the outside. She wished to be identified in this way and she gloried in her strength.

She was dressed in grey flowing robes and grey hood which, when in shadow, sometimes looked like a hat. She whirled it around herself wherever she went, that garment which was really there to hide her.

Abdullah had firm roots in the nomadic culture, but she was unhappy about her secondary female role. And, due to her upbringing, she did not countenance the freewheeling power of females either, for that matter. So she took a part that she had invented for herself: all the trimmings of being modest, but at the same time acting as a powerful female force.

She thought Owen ideal. To him, the often contradictory endgame had no purpose.

Owen had been revolutionized by the desire for Western culture to be a dominating influence over developments in the Middle East. He had newly developed doubts concerning how nations were governed on every continent. He wanted boundless freedom like in the wanderings of the nomadic desert tribes. But then he realized he was too self-centred to study other cultures in depth. He knew this was needed—even sought after by those who valued equality. But he didn't feel principles were anything he could sort out.

Instead, he became acute in finessing his own advantage. He was good at delivering weapons where needed. There were many opportunities for him to make enormous profits.

Abdullah went along with Owen's selfish visions, but she used the money she gained as she took up smuggling to help revolutionaries that opened up women's abilities to be more self-determining. She accommodated Owen because he was an efficient man.

She and Owen had assembled their cache of money and weaponry in the security of the Temple of Apollo, then upwards in the valley to Alfred's Tower. They were transferring their ill-gotten goods slowly through the woods and then from the tower to the distant, but urban and metropolitan Bath; and then as quickly as possible, they were to be transported out of Britain, via Bristol and the Bristol Channel.

In the Middle East everything remained turbulent, particularly the disturbing reign of many disparate groups. The only means many groupings and their followers had was a noticeable and distinct means of armed resistance. Owen, above all, was not against making some hard cash along these lines—no matter the political proclamations and who wanted what.

Each one of them had quite forgotten how disparate the aims were and how democracy should be encouraged by more peaceful means. Peace was not one of their purposes.

They had never researched the fact that Henry Hoare the Magnificent remained disquieted throughout his life at the many wars fought by the British. Hoare's letters and papers documented the anxieties connected with the wars of his period, like the Scottish rebellion, the American Revolution, the threat to England by France and Spain.

Then there were the threats in the countryside itself; the stealing of fowl by setting them on fire 'to suffocate them' and taking sacks of turnips from the fields. If challenged by the owners of productive fields, thieves were threatened with their life.

For Abdulla and Owen the only value in Henry Hoare's valley was to hide their trade in the temples and of those, Apollo's was the best in which to start and gain momentum.

Alternatively, there was Alfred's Tower. Both structures were near a road and in them their weaponry supplies were hidden from view. In Apollo's Temple, the lead statues had been removed. They had become additions to the main house and were displayed there. The temple was therefore locked, but it was an easily picked lock.

Abdulla and Owen felt the temple lent itself well to temporary storage of cargoes, mainly weapons of war.

Having first studied medicine Owen had wanted to set things right for the weak and disabled, but cynicism and money-making got the better of him. He became a successful banker in hedge funds.

Abdulla had a past of diverse migrations. At one point she was even sent to college despite her gender. And Owen wore his Victorian outfit to try to establish the sombre presence that his personality of chancing it had often failed to provide; he only sounded very aggressive because he didn't believe in anything.

But mostly now, he trained in keeping quiet.

Abdulla stabilized him. Mitigated his dominance.

Owen turned over in his mind what Elizabeth might do with her intense interest and knowledge of Stourhead. He suspected she was a moralist of the sort that lost sight of what a good deal of money meant; those dedicated to bicycles and peace usually were what he called eccentric.

Better fob her off and yet keep an eye on her.

The seemingly young financial expert was catching up with the loosely-robed Arabian female insurgent. They were now travelling the road from Apollo's Temple to Alfred's Tower.

They were both treading last year's leaves. These were brown and crinkly underfoot. Few people trespassed under the trees planted carefully for their native or—in past centuries—their American heritage. Many were imported firs, oaks or beeches.

As the beech trees were late coming into leaf, Abdullah and Owen were most exposed beneath their thick buds and scrolled bright green. But they shuffled through last season's discarded and dry leaves under which little grew. The disparate human smugglers made for the firs, dark and evergreen. They hoped no one would notice them there.

Owen was close to Abdulla. The wrapped parcel Abdulla was so carefully carrying was a small weapons parcel, but hidden in a carpet. She balanced it precariously above the many leaves and tree roots.

Owen spoke about his belief that the weapons were secure. "Alfred's Tower has good roomy cellars under the stairs, and we'll deposit all there. Then we'll leave for Bath and have the ship arranged for the Bristol Channel. That will be the easier part.

"Elizabeth, the female scholar, is wrapped up in herself, but I'll keep an eye on her.

"The German police inspector has little power on non-native turf. Besides, he is on holiday, and doesn't wish any involvement in police work.

"I'm surprised he doesn't get bored. But Germans are startlingly single-minded, once they begin to want to know. How I'd hate to be in his shoes."

Abdullah didn't answer. She was concentrating on putting each foot right and not stumbling. The wrapping of fine patterned grey carpet was alright under the beeches, but would be revealed if the top barrels of the guns were to be seen gleaming in front of the needles of the low evergreen branches.

ELIZABETH WAS EXPLAINING how important it was to acknowledge Apollo as the patron of arts. He was not just the god who drove the heavenly sun chariot, but who sagaciously evoked feelings by means of knowing the arts. He raised emotions through it. Either you liked what art invented or abhorred it.

"Apollo," she was saying, "is the idol of art. The sun god with his chariot keeps his inspiration for the hard work of painters and yet he speaks in the cryptic terms of his place of worship, Delos. He will tell you about the future, but in riddles, which sounds so much better if you are able to decipher his predictions. For example, if he utters the ambiguous words, words like 'I will remain a secret', what does he mean by this and what are you to do?"

James Owen, in her recollection, had hemmed and hawed. The Inspector went to the point. "He means: search out my mystery."

Queberon stood still, suddenly inspired. He began tracing the still extant footprints of what he thought of as the spooky apparition in woollen grey. The footprints led to a door. The Inspector put an eye to the murky inner view of the temple. He inspected everything minutely and saw suspicious looking protectively wrapped packages. They were of a size and shape that suggested assault rifles like the Russian Kalashnikov or German Heckler and Koch. All were neatly stacked in dark corners.

"Does the National Trust sometimes keep various things, like for example hunting rifles, on their property?" he asked Elizabeth. He saw white shapes in oil-stained wrappings. He had thought the Trust an organisation exclusively dedicated to preserving heritage.

"How absurd," said James Owen, who had suddenly appeared and was poking his black-tufted head back around the raised base of Apollo's Temple. He was keeping his eyes on them. But he pulled out his gold watch and chain and said he was just returning to the Spread Eagle Inn and was in a hurry.

His last words, before he took the path down through the rocks where the old hermitage used to be, were, "I wouldn't rummage around in old temples if I were you. They look fine from the outside but tend to be musty within. Enjoy the view into the valley with the bright rhododendrons. Such good weather."

As they watched Owen walking away, getting smaller and smaller, Elizabeth remarked that he seemed to be chased by devils. These very un-Grecian spirits were reducing him to a blot on the landscape. He swirled away in black shadows.

She changed the subject. She wanted to emphasise where they were, the sacredness of the landscape. She had been wishing that the Inspector could envision this eighteenth-century precept of the landscape garden as the 'genius of the place'. This was mentioned by Alexander Pope and emphasized so much since then as a valid design principle for the new naturalistic landscape garden.

"But it was more than that," she went on to insist, "on a deep level it is connected with the sacred grove, the place which spirits inhabit.

"Landscape has a direct influence on mood. We walk into it, but how it is structured in writing and painting has in addition power to create psychological experience. Landscape gardens delight in temples and features, and the country house extends this reading of a place 'out of time', 'long ago and far away', the commonplace of fairy stories.

"Henry Hoare was, by his own account, educating himself, and therefore participating in the world created by painting, poetry, and gardening. This alternative world was one in which he delighted and with which he let his children and friends become familiar, to allow them, as well, to wander in this beauty which countered destruction and discord."

Elizabeth maintained there must be room for living hope and high ideals in the world. Even though these were not often expressed enough and rarely voiced aloud, they were effective as a way forward. She wanted to struggle on with presenting her view of the ideal, thinking it must result in change. A person may not live up to such perfection, but trying would increase goodness, Elizabeth thought. Not everyone would agree with her.

Inspector Queberon found her view to be too rarefied, since in his mind the future was bound to be bumpier and narrower. Especially when it came to politics and practical endeavours, it was hard to maintain hopes of the ideal. One had to make the best of what was proposed. Only the determined could advance their ideals, like those like Elizabeth that believed humankind must secure values beyond selfishness. Ideals of goodness were oftentimes thwarted—or could they be realized by persuading others? Only in very exceptional circumstances, he thought.

Elizabeth and Inspector Queberon were ready to set out for the longer trip around the lake, through the grotto, and up the path to the Pantheon. They had taken the steep upward path to Apollo's Temple; now they proceeded on the way around the lake.

THE PANTHEON

As they walked, the Inspector invited Elizabeth to speak at length about the connection of the gods to the garden. He wanted to understand the great eighteenth-century quest for morality and righteousness embedded in this landscape garden. The stories were decipherable by her, but mute to him, cast as they were in ornament and statue.

The route they had now chosen went past the Pantheon at a distance and then up to it, firstly around the lake and then entering the grotto. And thus they came to thoroughly appreciate how effective it was to dam the Stour River. The trees that ringed the lake made the grotto and Pantheon shine against the green. And below the Pantheon the grotto was designed as the rusticated 'eye'. It looked out over the waters of the lake dug out with much labour. The lake waters were smooth as if floating in space, a bar between heaven and the world below. There were clouds reflected in the waters but, more than that, the lake, with its smoothness, also hinted at the phantom nether realm below it where other pictures were lost.

Elizabeth thought sorrowfully of the white Chinese bridge on the farthest, northern corner of the lake. Now only present in her mind, it was compensated by the beauty of the many trees that excited their minds. They continued and rounded the lake.

They wanted to visit the grotto of the River God.

To their right was the hill down which the springs of the Stour River bounded. Some of the waters which bubbled up subsequently poured reverently into the pool over which the nymph presided.

The nymph was in her cave, and the waters entered the underground edifice behind and beneath her, showing her reclining figure in the subdued light of the grotto. She shared it with the River God. He was in the next underground room. Her message which was inscribed in stone for all visitors to see, was cast in the same words as Alexander Pope carved on his own grotto at Twickenham next to the Thames. Inscribed were the same words:

"Nymph of the Grot these sacred springs I keep
And to the murmur of these waters sleep;
Ah! Spare my slumbers, gently tread the cave
And drink in silence or in silence lave."

Elizabeth was steeped in the lore of the gods which the banker who had designed Stourhead in the eighteenth century knew so well. She imparted to the Inspector the myths that were renewed here. She said: "Apollo, the mighty sun god you just visited, took a branch from the bay trees growing in Tempe and began the tradition of young men returning every nine years to gather crowns of laurel and offer sacrifice. They returned each year in a procession to Apollo's Delphic shrine.

"Thus the Vale of Tempe is grounded several times over in the leitmotifs that are repeated in the landscape garden: in its sacred and Arcadian topography, its tie to Apollo and his myths of illumination and mystery.

"These waters are beneficial to whoever bathes in them, being extremely invigorating. The most melodious birds keep singing everywhere and delight the traveller. The nymph is the daughter of the River God Peneios. She is the beloved Daphne."

Elizabeth absolutely did not want him to miss out on the messages that were inherent in this rocky underworld. So much so that she gripped his hand quite firmly. Such a pleasant and unexpected touching of their hands surprised both of them. And he responded. His hand enclosed hers, holding tight, and he didn't want to let go. He seemed to cradle her warm hand in his. She stepped closer, her hold like a sweet flower in spring that was about to open.

Elizabeth quickly glanced away; yet her eyes had a new and captivating sparkle. Horatio glanced down; modesty reigned, yet he saw himself confronting his desire welling up—a sensation reaching into his consciousness.

She was almost whispering now. "The River God himself, according to Ovid, was 'seated in a cave of overhanging rock; he was giving laws to his waters and to his nymphs'.

"The sacred place can suspend actual time or reality. Entering can elicit wonder and engagement. Normal life is suspended in order to appreciate another world."

The Inspector was charmed by the warmth and —dare he assume—the double meaning of Elizabeth's words. He raptly took them in; he tasted their significance.

The opening from the 'eye' of the rocky cavern with its sightline to the village married together all the different parts—it made Stourhead whole, like Elizabeth's voice straining all her knowledge to keep him happy in the landscape garden where he had only come to get away from it all. In this place his sterile past made fun of him.

But he was gaining in his attentiveness outside his police chores. He praised the prowess and virtues of the gods and more than ever their positive intervention and possibly how they could fashion his future.

From its 'eye' to the village, the River God and the Nymph encompassed the view of the medieval church and the inn. This sightline emphasized time through the ages. And it included the immediate watery domain, the lake, opposite, before the eyes lifted to the buildings and the shifting ripples where the god Neptune reigned.

The woodland and the bridge spoke of open-ended adventure. In his mind Queberon was lost in thought, walking and imbibing the twists and turns that life could bring. He was aware of a new readiness to engage.

Elizabeth, he saw, was now pointing to the white, bearded figure beyond the first rocky chamber. She especially wished him to focus on what he saw as they approached. Here was the River God. Some thought this god should have an oar in his hand; and indeed, the River God Thames did.

But the River God Stour was pointing upwards with his finger. His white, gnarled hand made it plain that he meant Elizabeth and the Inspector to climb the twisting, fern overhung and woody path upwards.

And they set out.

At the River God's side, the pottery jar spilled fertile water downriver into the lake, but his direct look was at Elizabeth and the Inspector. He was indicating as they moved towards him that he wanted their footsteps up from the Underworld towards the Light. Emotion, he seemed to indicate, is empathetic. Feeling is what water indicates as it flows.

It meant taking all their wishes into the reality of life.

They realized the beauty of the Pantheon, half-hidden in trees.

It too had an 'eye', but it was an opening to the ever changing sky. It was the Pantheon's opeion. Beyond it lay the action of the gods and conjecture.

Within, under the 'eye', were the gods that were significant to Henry Hoare. Foremost was Hercules. Then there were the female goddesses, Ceres and Isis, one the goddess of harvests and summer; the other, the goddess mother of us all.

Henry Hoare had added in the female line St. Susanna to remind him of his wife, Susan, and of his daughter, Susanna. Both had predeceased him. Here in the niches of the Pantheon was their memorial.

But he had also lined up the other gods. And they were good company. Hercules had triumphed with his many tasks, superhuman and difficult. He was human but he was also a god. It let him span both worlds. This was his central role in the Pantheon. The semi-god who performed his tasks. He reminded Hoare of the 'Herculean' travails that all who aspired to the good must undergo.

Elizabeth and the Inspector walked around and around this and the other statues, admiring their beauty. They shone in contrast against the oxblood reddish walls. They were set on pedestals and taller than humans.

The Inspector went round every one. He was particularly taken by Diana with her bow. This virgin goddess, the sister of Apollo, was guardian of the woods. He looked at her raised arm and lowered bow. She was striding forwards.

Then he noticed something. Secreted behind her pedestal were packets, neat, but ready to be lifted in an instant. They were more numerous than the ones he had thought he had seen in the murky depths of the Apollo Temple. They included glittery ones shining through their outer coverings and more strident looking ones that the Inspector thought were more in line with weapons.

The Pantheon was being used for other things

than visitors contemplating the virtues of the gods, or so it seemed.

Elizabeth gasped and said angrily, "I won't rest until we are rid of this violence. And I hope the goddess Diana carries her bow for the hunt."

IN THE HANGING WOOD

Rather than fingerprint the wrappings immediately—and the Inspector had friends in the police service in Wiltshire—the pair went out into Diana's hunting grounds.

They implicitly agreed that there could be no better stirring pursuit of criminals than a dedicated woman who knew Stourhead and an instinctive and well-versed detective inspector.

They skirted around the Pantheon and found tracks. The leaf mould had been left pristine by the winter cold and now, in spring, besides the varied animal tracks, had registered human and recent scuff marks. These seemed to have been made by two different pairs of boots scuttling through them.

The trail led from the crushed leaves into the dense planting beyond, but the boot marks were close together like an intimate collaboration. It had been early morning. The leaves bore witness to disturbance with mud kicked up which was barely dried.

Elizabeth followed the footsteps in a northerly direction. She suspected she was going into the woods towards Alfred's Tower.

The Inspector's attention was focussed on the ground. He saw where an object had repeatedly come to rest. It was accompanied by a few strands of light grey wool.

They went forward following the marks the culprits had left, caught now and again by branches. They ducked but continued uphill. Now they found a path. It was easier to walk, but even though the ground changed, it still featured the footprints. They straightened and bowed. They inched their way forward. Two dogs hunting in a pack would not be a poor analogy.

But Elizabeth saw, sauntering down the path in her direction, a man whose dark clothes and waistcoat looked vaguely familiar. She straightened and stood still, wanting a closer look. The Inspector didn't move either, only taking the occasion to square his shoulders and tidy his tie, jacket and shirt.

"I thought James Owen vanished far too quickly," murmured Elizabeth. "I wonder what he's still doing here, and so far out towards the Six Wells too."

The figure took shape. He was in full regalia. Black trousers, gold chain, white shirt, waistcoat, with no buttons on the collar of his shirt, sombre tie. He descended the path. When he was close, he hailed Elizabeth.

"I've mislaid my credit cards for the bank. I think I may have left them at the Spread Eagle. Do you think someone may have found them and left them at Reception?"

He glanced at Elizabeth. The clothes that made him sombre as a clergyman hung loosely about him.

"Please come and vouch for me at the inn. Your companion here could spare you a while. I'm sure a lady like you will make a difference. I am so pleased I happened upon you."

Elizabeth was an optimist and hoped for conversion of evil to good. She wanted a change, even in Owen. And she loved to be needed. Maybe Owen merited being given a second chance. And perhaps rivalry to the Inspector could elicit firm commitment and excite tension provoked by a hint of the proverbial love triangle! Even if she hated Owen—such strong emotions!—yes, that would finalize disgust for Owen or love for Horatio.

And the Inspector's emotions certainly surged. His heartbeat choked him.

Elizabeth said she would be back within the hour. She would just help Owen out. Then they would resume their "mutual pleasure in landscape gardens."

Inspector Queberon was left to shuffle through the leaves of last year's autumn, shrivelled and brown, to think upon what he might want for the future. He was at a loss. And emotionally he was a man in turmoil.

So suddenly abandoned, he saw how he had enjoyed learning so much about Stourhead without lifting a finger. And simultaneously he knew how completely he envisioned himself drawing Elizabeth close to him. He realized suddenly why he had eyed her so intently. He was more than just drawn to her. He was in love. He missed her company acutely. He did not wish to pursue Stourhead's meanings without her.

Then he looked down. He glanced at the footsteps Elizabeth and Owen had made in leaving together.

He looked again to the footprints, intending to use his time slowly.

The man's imprint stood out.

These were just like the pair of boots he and Elizabeth had been following. Inspector Queberon stared.

He had to contend with his feelings of distrust

for Owen. This emotion came upon him like a stomach upset. He could either blame a sudden irrational twinge or admit to his being in love, but was he seeing things in identifying these footprints. Was he being prejudiced, sloppy, ill-judged? Could these be anyone's size 6 footprints?

He looked at the heel. He looked at the distinct toe-marks.

He could see in the distance the two heads bobbing down the valley. They were far away, yet close.

Suddenly he was afraid for Elizabeth. He acknowledged his involvement, his entanglement; he wasn't going to shy away, return to objectivity, pretending he didn't care.

He started to run downhill where Elizabeth had gone.

He would catch up; make sure she was safe.

He lost sight of them on the winding and uneven path and because of the many low branches and the twist and turns.

Near Flora's Temple he noticed a splashing and floundering as if someone had lost their footing and plunged into the lake.

All he could see, and he was out of breath now, was wet hair floating on the surface. Too many waves and brown fizziness and streaks of untidy flotsam and jetsam were pitching about in uneven water. The floor of the lake was filled with rocks and uneven, sunken objects.

Shadows and arms flailing were all he could make out. Was a young man there who'd slipped and lost his footing? There were unaccounted for ambling young men exercising. The poor floundering person that was nearly submerged was having a terrible time trying to come upright.

The Inspector dived in. He was able to grasp a collar, then a soft shirt. He stabilized himself by gaining strong footage.

But it was not a young man he had in his arms; it was Elizabeth.

She was spluttering. He was muscular enough to heave her sideways, and onto the verge.

She was beside herself; spitting water. Her reaction to despair and possible drowning was rage. When she began to make sense, she instinctively railed. She turned against her thoughts of anyone trying to be peaceful, to placate. Her view of Owen was exactly what Rosalinde had pointed out.

She frothed at her mouth and shook in her wet clothes. They were streaming and flapping around her bust and hips. With her clothes clinging to her she looked as curvaceous as a Greek statue, draped nicely.

The Inspector gave her his coat.

He was moved; had she thrashed further, she would have courted death.

She garbled bad things about Owen. That Victorian man had deceived her good intentions towards him. Had pushed her, had calculated the moment and had thrown her to die in the water. He had chosen a place where her feet would slip, over and over, and she would lose her breath and the struggle to surface.

"He wanted me to drown! He wanted to be rid of me! He wanted me to lie with the fish, with that water-drinking, wave-commanding, non-existent Neptune!"

She was dripping wet and shaking. Yet on the bank, finally, she regained control. In a trembling voice, she tried to establish composure.

The Inspector spoke soothingly. She told him, venting her strong feeling, and in no uncertain terms that she could like to have Owen throttled.

She was an angry Scotswoman and there were no two ways about it. She would change clothes immediately and confront this villain.

Inspector Queberon, who was both gentleman and deeply touched, steered her to the Spread Eagle Inn.

IN HONOUR OF ALFRED'S TOWER

Liberty, above so much else, was inscribed on the distant Tower that was designated as the one dedicated to Alfred. This was the Alfred of medieval allure, who had raised his standard against the invading Danes on this spot, and who Henry Hoare had chosen to honour.

It was up the valley. Miles of Wiltshire were to be seen from its top. But within its walls were hidden the many weapons Abdullah and Owen had acquired.

Abdullah was busy seeing to all that. She and Owen were ready to have them transported, but she was also very carefully putting down her weapons load, cradled as if it were her baby. The good thing about the weapons was their relative non-descriptive nature. As soon as she had the means to ship them to the Middle East, the part of the world which was in such a contentious state, she would stop eyeing them over and over; and stop seeing nothing but suspects and opponents. She was jumpy, even though Stourhead was a quiet corner; the very reason they had chosen it. No suspicious and overly curious people came here to nose around. But she remained apprehensive, unwilling to shoulder this mission without her accomplice.

Her English counterpart was late; he had promised to aid the stashing and hiding of weaponry. He had obtained most of them from a corrupt official from Porton Down, not so far from here. Their trade had been obtrusive enough that they had slipped weaponry through Stourhead for many months undetected and gradually amassed quite a cache. Each sojourn through the landscape garden had added to their stockpiling. They were to distribute the weapons in boatloads to young men engaged in fighting against oligarchs—or at least, that's what they said.

Abdullah thought Owen should take sides; in fact, she hoped he would. If he was going to sell weapons, it did matter to whom. But it was hard to know which side he was on. There was something contradictory in his clean living and dirty dealing. She, on the other hand, would fight for anyone advancing women's rights. She believed change had to happen.

But Owen was nowhere to be seen.

ELIZABETH all but dragged Inspector Queberon to the top of the valley, opposite Alfred's Tower, such a good vantage point for overseeing what was happening in the landscape garden.

She wanted to scour for the suspicious Owen and any of his accomplices from the tree-shaded walk that was placed on the same high level as Alfred's Tower. They could view the Tower and all its terrain from this point. It was a good observation point. She wanted to have a view of her adversaries on the plateau that was etched there above the dip to the Tower.

Here she could see all of the valley and the upper reaches to Alfred's Tower and beyond. Henry Hoare had frequented this hill above the valley, as he took his horseback ride behind the manor house. He had planted the ride there with firs, now cut down and replaced by beeches. At the end of the ride he had built an Obelisk with a disc to reflect the eastern, rising sun. This too had been replaced, but merely with another Obelisk. Now the sun-disc and the Obelisk held sway once more over the countryside. And it stood facing Alfred's Tower.

The Obelisk was supposed to triumph over Alfred's Tower. It sparkled every time the sun rose and said to all, here is the sun that is such an important sign of Christian faith. The Obelisk reigned as the ancient sign of resurrection. It was another aspect with which Henry Hoare brought the world of his Christian faith into alignment with the virtues of the gods in Stourhead. He added this Obelisk as a sign he would often encounter by way of his faith in crediting the invisible world. He honoured the pagan gods and the Obelisk and the integration of gods and Christians. Henry Hoare stated very strongly in his landscape garden that both were important to him.

Elizabeth stood at the base of the Obelisk with the Inspector. They looked at the far tower that indicated Liberty to all, no matter where they came from, especially when they walked these shores. That idea had become foremost and showed what Alfred's Tower was meant to convey.

Elizabeth and Horatio plunged down the slope from the Obelisk toward the three-sided edifice of solid brick soon enough. In the meantime, Elizabeth swore to uphold the peacefulness that Stourhead was happy to acknowledge because it combined the sacredness of pagan and Christian virtues. She let go of her anger, wanting justice to reign over war and its killing weaponry.

She egged on Inspector Queberon, hoping that his police powers would complement both her wanting justice and her quelling of anger—although her angry feeling cropped up now and again, even though she was straining for justice not revenge. She trusted Queberon. His observation and deduction would reveal the subversion that was undoubtedly occurring in the landscape garden before their very eyes. They were hurrying towards Alfred's Tower. This must be where Owen was hiding.

She said, "For the sake of direction take the same view as from the Obelisk, remembering the trunks of the trees that stand tall and reflect how the sun shines. The trunks will always show the sun the same way the Obelisk does. They shine and give us direction, flickering with the light of the sun even now when it is setting in the west.

"The culprit wanted me dead. His vehicle is still in the car park, so he will be afoot in these hills. Keep a keen watch for the black suit jacket and black trousers. He can't hide before dark—and he'll certainly have problems where there are no streetlights."

With an intake of breath, the Inspector said, "I'll climb down between the trees. Owen is bound to come up the valley, probably up to the Six Wells. But I won't try to apprehend him, just tail him, since he must be hiding his real intent. Although with these English draperies I'm wearing, he's bound to see me first."

They looked once more over the valley of the gods and the distance to Alfred's Tower and its proclamation of liberty. This is what they believed in: working together. It was their motive now.

They were in love.

They began their descent into the woods, hidden by the unfurling green leaves and the pale trunks of woodland which had long been used to secrets. Were it not for the light they knew was coming from the west, they would have been lost. The descent was steep and treacherous.

Elizabeth and the Inspector soon fanned out. Barely visible to one another within the twisted, hanging wood of the beeches, they scurried forward. The light now barely touched the westward bark of the trees.

In between the pale, straightening trunks, far, then near, weaving in and out, but making its presence known, was a shimmer of white. Not shy, not more than tangible, was the shadow of a mythic, definitive presence. It was Diana herself.

She was armed with her bow and arrow. Behind her, as sparks of light, almost like lichen luminous on trees, were her nymphs. Diana was out hunting. She was running, fleet of foot, glowing white and nimble, towards the pond named after her. She was lighter than all the unfurling leaves, and she passed through all the shining trunks of beech, awaiting the moon and her perfect reflection. She was the Diana of Lake Avernus. She was the Diana of Lake Nemi. She was the moon, and not the moon; she was her double, and not her double. She was a shining, hunting, presence.

Elizabeth and the Inspector saw her only as the rising May moon, high above and now visible and now not visible through the strong branches of the trees.

The sun had set. The moon was silver and round.

There were the two of them. Then there was a black shape far ahead. Then there was the marbled Diana, white and luminous, wanting her will done, and commanding her troops. The chase was on.

James Owen was walking fast—half running—through the woods. He was bent on reaching Alfred's Tower quick as a flash and conversing with Abdullah. He did not look behind him.

He was angry at the many leaves through which he trod. Kicking and swearing under his breath, he wanted no sliding or impediments. Yet the beeches were like elephant's trunks snorkelling into the ground where ever he went. They wanted to trip him up. The roots lay in wait, all innocent, curving into the ground, silent under emerging leaves, black, thick, and treacherous. The daunting, shifting light did its part. Here and there the moon, all in lustred silver, shone brightly, and let the trees cast a dark shadow.

Owen slipped and slithered. Then he straightened. Diana took another shot. Where her arrow landed, another black rootling grasped the earth and sought to cover itself in soil and leaves. The trees were alive. They swayed gently to make way for their favourite goddess. And they continued to stick their roots and elephantine twisting and clutching into the ground, looping like coiled rods hidden by last year's leaves. It was done in the whole hanging wood, so it seemed natural. Frustrated that he was not going forward, Owen slid. He landed on his belly, crawling. Leaves were smeared onto his Victorian clothing. They seemed as innocuous as last year's brown leaves, decayed and decrepit. The high, emerging green leaves smiled down and waved him on.

The beeches leapt in triumph around him. They were dancing. The moon swung with them. It was singing its favourite song, a lullaby.

Owen struggled to his feet. And down he went again. It was hard to progress.

Finally he hugged a beech tree. He clawed at it and hung on. He knocked it with his forehead as if he wanted to make sense prevail once more. The tree was on the edge, and as Owen let go again, he stumbled out of the woods. Before him was open, hilly country. He saw Alfred's Tower.

He ran towards it and his mission and Abdullah.

As he gave the knock agreed upon, Abdullah opened the door. Abdullah gazed in wonder at the ragged, tall man.

"Where have you been; you are looking like someone who got kicked and then rolled in last year's leaves. And you are late," she said.

"Never seemed to end, that loathsome return from the rim," replied Owen. "This valley is at the beck and call of the weirdest machinations."

Diana had given a last glance towards the Tower. Now her attention was on the moon. She would need some collaboration.

Her turning to Ceres was in this vein. The goddess of the coming fullness of summer would have a say. Ceres of the Pantheon here in Stourhead would see how Abdullah and Owen could be splattered and look silly. These two had, after all, mocked the gods.

Ceres was of the mind flowers could grow in each single weapon, no matter what kind. Not so long ago, the hippies had sung of it. They had sung "No more war" and it had reverberated. Or, she suggested, how about the fertile rain of spring putting weapons out of action by waterlogging? Thus thought the ever-fertile Ceres.

Weapons, with their long barrels, their crosshairs, their handles, on the whole, could work by their very construction on how the goddesses conceived contamination, she was sure of it. "Diana, my sweet goddess, sister of Apollo, I do not think we are short of means." They were good at working together.

LOST BUT FOUND

The woods were dim but the beeches visible, as Elizabeth and the Inspector gathered together once more. Dim was rather an overstatement as the beeches were grey-barked and then black and the cast-off leaves on the ground discernible only where the moon let their rough curling corpses shine intermittently. Occasionally the full moon glinted in strong light as the branches gave way. The grasses glinted like swords in the moonlight around the Obelisk.

Elizabeth and the Inspector were now back across the valley, descending the path from the Obelisk back to the Spread Eagle Inn. They left behind the Obelisk now reflecting the cool light of the moon from its disc at the top. The grass was turning wet from dew, in silvery spears, pointing upwards.

As they drew near the statue of Apollo at the end of the terrace, they began to appreciate the onset of this clear magnificent night.

Elizabeth, getting her breath back, reminisced on the magnificent moonlit nights of Mull. She went into a reverie, praising the dark sea with its shining waves. She was, after all, used to the pearly light of the moon reflected on the waters. What she thought most splendid, was the rising and dual character of the moon high in the sky and, at the same time, swimming in the waters. Not only did it lustre the sky in its transit, but the moon also showed its face in various shapes as it rested in the waters.

The sea on Mull was stationary and bright, and the moon was a shining, luminous circle, but a minute later, it was swimming up and down in the waves. The essence of its movement was its glorious face emerging, expected, and often distorted in the bright waves. And sometimes it disappeared.

There on Mull, the moon would complete its high arc over the mountains of the island. And because of its dual nature it would lie down to swim in the Sound, where Lismore Island, the Sound of Mull, and the sea going towards Oban met. She loved that moon. She had walked many a night to see it. She had told many stories of a kindly moon disposed so well towards Islanders.

She wanted the Inspector to listen. She was intent on catching his attention. She needed him even though she wouldn't admit it. She wouldn't admit, either, that she was thinking about the glories of Mull in the light of the full moon in order to distract herself from giving up on their chase.

The Inspector was in a quandary. He was reaching decisions. He was in the dark and then in the light much as the full moon, which was glowing bright and the next minute hidden by a cloud. And as he contemplated, he looked once more at the pale white and black grid of shadows the beech avenue cast in front of them.

What better night to challenge Eizabeth's strict code of high and mighty aloofness, he thought. Would she be more open, more than a friend to him? He considered himself to be a stranger even though he was someone she knew from her many contacts with him in Dessau. But that had been in a country foreign to her—and in his capacity as an inspector of police. What would she think of him now? Now or never, he thought.

Inspector Queberon tentatively asked whether she could think of this pearly object in heaven as their good omen, given them by the powers of Stourhead? Shining in full-faced splendour, the moon countenanced their working together? A token, this moon was, like a magic coin, suddenly precious to them and ferrying them to landscapes where peacefulness and cooperation between them was delightful?

Elizabeth was happy observing the full moon; but suddenly she was aware the Inspector was talking to her more intimately, was confessing his regard. Here was a normally attentive, self-sufficient man going mad.

It must be the moon, the clear night, and Apollo, the god of art, which made him effusive.

But suddenly she too was inclined to be less stand-offish.

He was neat and brainy. Inclining toward the mad or mental was never her view of right-minded detective inspectors. So, really, she had to place him in the category of sane men.

Taking the down-to-earth view, they were like peas in a pod, people who were in love. Except that the nature of their occupations and how they behaved, had kept them separate like chalk and cheese.

Now the moon, or was it Artemis, or was it Diana, let surprising thoughts occupy them. They leaned against each other. Warmth was mutual and they hugged each other. They dropped their inhibitions and proceeded in unison. The Inspector carefully guided Elizabeth across the lawn, taking her arm.

They descended and passed by the library of Sir

Richard Colt-Hoare, the inheritor of Stourhead. This nephew had not changed the gardens, keeping all in pristine order. He had also surveyed the ancient heritage of Britain in Stone Circles and Henges and Druids. Magic was part of the British legacy. It had captured Elizabeth to use her Second Sight as insight, letting intuition add to her feelings. She was now intoxicated, her vast academic knowledge of place only a first step on the ladder to heaven. The Inspector's knowledge, too, was an attribute suddenly confronted. It had served him well, but it was nothing like magic. He became joyfully irrational.

Still in place, but benign and outspoken, were the landscapes painted in Nature. This made the gliding into love part of Nature into Art, at last purposeful yet natural. The evening light and the smooth-stone temples were the century's favourite subjects in the paintings of landscapes. Lorrain and Poussin, both admired in the eighteenth century, used their landscape paintings to evoke anew the feeling that grew so passionately at the time, that Nature was enriched with man-made design. The scale of knowing how to express Art was the feeling also nascent in Nature.

The landscape was conceived so that whoever came, walked in the glories of the valley of the gods. In the gloriously moonlit night, Elizabeth and Queberon seemed to glide above the earth. The Pantheon was surreal in the moonlight in the midst of the hugging, mint-green, sprouting, many-branched trees. Elizabeth and the Inspector were no longer returning to an inn in a National Trust landscape garden, they were walking in the mythical and the poetic, star-struck under the luminous moon.

The mood lasted even to the empty tables spread in the courtyard of the Spread Eagle Inn. The Inspector stepped beyond these to a view of the Bristol Cross and St. Peter's Church. He took Elizabeth possessively in his charge. Their shadows merged.

Both viewed the emblems of old England. Both saw the Palladian bridge in full splendour before them. Above them, above the trees and lit by heavenly light, together with the full moon, were the rotating stars, some grouped in constellations attributed to the gods.

It was an anomaly, the medieval Church and the Greco-Roman gods, but Stourhead was one of the few places that brought opposite realities into alignment.

ESCAPE

Abdullah cast an eye over the mud-spattered James Owen. She was surprised at the dishevelment, so unusual in a man of pristine, even fastidious, habits.

For Owen weapon smuggling had come to be a regular pastime. He didn't care who was injured as the victim or who lost a life because of his trade in weaponry. Owen subscribed to the philosophy of gain and not loss. He was pragmatic only in selling to causes. These were interchangeable. And Stourhead was ideal and convenient for the assembly and onward shipment of his lethal but lucrative wares.

Owen worked with hard and fast objectives. He dealt in tangible, material things. Material things were efficient, repaid him, and were a means to an end. Or, in other words, when push came to shove more money was produced for his coffers.

So far, everything had gone well. Then, all of a sudden, Professor Elizabeth Hammerstein had appeared, and with her a detective inspector from foreign parts, keen-eyed and intent on exploring Stourhead. What was more, both of them took pleasure in noticing detail and were not lightly distracted.

This had registered in both their minds, Abdullah as well as Owen, as being worthy of watchfulness. But it was only one thing on their minds. They were being beset by other woes. They had immediate troubles which were hard to explain. One of these was how on earth wet patches appeared all over them as if by magic.

Abdulla looked disapprovingly at Owen, who looked disconcertedly back at her.

Both had sodden patches on their outfits and walking boots.

In no time, these wet and intractable spots that appeared on their clothing began sprouting vegetation. It was spring and winter wheat and ivy that shot up in fresh green.

Owen was being covered in ivy. Tendrils of it slipped inward towards his underwear. Ivy leaves of the mottled kind showed down his suit jacket sleeves. His trousers were blotted in rip-tides of heart-shaped ivy of completely darkened hue. The vegetation was growing everywhere, and hugging, and throttling. It was like snakes bent on choking every breath out of their victims.

Owen tried shaking and tap-dancing to get rid of the ivy.

Abdullah was about to laugh when the wheat grew overlong shafts up her wide grey skirts, then up her chest and then gathered like a necklace around her collarbone. She was beginning to look like a bundle of ready-to-harvest wheat. She could barely manage her long hair and carefully crafted black scarf under the grey hood which hid her identity as she prickled with golden, growing wheat.

Even the weapons, all the carefully assembled guns, had developed sudden and unexpected puddles of wet, and they were mired in sheaves of wheat.

All of a sudden there was a knock on the door of Alfred's Tower. Abdullah and Owen brushed leaves and wheat from their clothes and after a short delay opened the door. The vegetation grew back despite their efforts, but nonetheless they peered to see who was coming to visit. Abdullah was foremost and she opened the door. What they saw outside was a wizened old woman, a charming old lady.

"I am Grandma Gretel," the old woman with a stick said. "How wonderful you both look."

"I think I'll come in," she continued. "Did you have a good time in the woods? I sometimes live in this Tower and just came to see how it is. I like its steep staircase and its view."

The conversation disconcerted the two smugglers. It verged on the convivial and they could do without it right now. How to get rid of her, they thought, almost in unison. All Owen could come up with was: "How nice."

"You must both have run into my other friend Ceres, old dear. She does so well in handling wheat, not to speak of the evergreen ivy. Summer is her season. Everything grows. Poor dear, she lost her child, Persephone, to winter cold. Poor, poor thing. But she gets livelier as soon as spring comes. Let me see how nicely the ivy cascades out from your collar and sleeve. And then, let me also see more of your growth of wheat!"

So continued the indomitable, charming old lady.

The vegetation was now shifting over to cover whatever the two carried with them. They suddenly had nice bearded growths on clothes, weapons, jewels. The metal and triggers of the guns were a bronze, golden colour, the colour of harvest wheat. The ivy, on the other hand, was climbing down the gun's muzzles, choking them.

The two were watching helplessly. They knew at

least the wheat was too early. This was springtime. The growth rate seemed mysterious, too. The whole Tower was being filled. The birds, as well now, seemed to congregate. They liked the sudden appearance of blackberries on the ivy. Nesting and eating were their pleasures.

Abdullah said tentatively to the old lady, "I will offer to bring you back home, if you want. Don't you want to enjoy your fire in the snug fireplace; it's still cold, and you would have me attend to it, and I would help, and you could enjoy, and tell me your stories, and you don't really want to see Alfred's Tower, not really, in this weather, it is by far too bothersome for you, and trust me, go home with me nicely." And on she went in this vein, all a little too fast, but gaining in confidence and pushiness.

"My real name is Grandma Gretel Isis. I'm sure you've seen me often enough. I'm very much on my own, but capable although very venerable in my years," the old lady croaked. "But better you attend to my dear relative Ceres. Give her the libation of your weapons and she won't practice on you as to fields of wheat. And you had better throw out any notion of fights and calamities, as none of us like it."

Abdullah had heard of a past in which Isis had temples in the East. But was Isis a grandma? To Owen, Gretel sounded like a fairytale. Wasn't there a witch in it somewhere?

Apprehension took over. The old woman disappeared.

Owen said to Abdullah, "Very weird. Let's shoulder our goods and stash them and take the weapons in the car with their cloth wrappings. We can escape to Bristol. We can load the weapons on the boat in the harbour on the river Severn and go to sea from there."

"Yes, let's hurry, and rescue your car. We can cut the silly growth down as we go," replied Abdullah.

Owen, trailing his ivy, tried leaving. The ivy jerked him to the ground, and subsequently wrestled him against the wall. He swore abundantly.

Abdullah used shears to try to snip him free. She smelt of wheat fields and a wind tossed her about. She didn't know where it was coming from; certainly it wasn't coming from within the Tower.

They were both tough. And they proceeded, but under adversity.

Isis watched from the stronghold of her statue in the Parthenon.

She thought Ceres ingenious. Under the cover of statues, they directed the mayhem. They produced their adversaries' great desire for retreat. They were glad Henry Hoare selected them for the Pantheon. Isis really expected no less, since her lineage went back to ancient times and she had many temples, including one in the very heart of Rome.

The only private anomaly was Henry Hoare's statue of Susanna, but he had personal reasons to include her. And she was powerful in her own right.

Unaware of the goddesses, Owen fought his way down the slope in order to escape at last.

He became dizzy again in the beech wood. Not sure how or who it was that was trailing him, Owen reeled between the pale trunks. From one upward curving trunk to the next, he saw something white and sometimes an old-fashioned bow and arrow. Liquid smeared into his eyes. It seemed the sap was rising nicely and the twigs decided his eyes and face should gather it. He thought the sticky stuff just landed on him like bird droppings.

Owen was in a sorry state when he at last glimpsed his car. He blinked, wanting a clear view. It seemed just like he had left it.

He felt like a cat that had endured being brushed the wrong way. Nevertheless, he took possession of his car in the parking lot of the Spread Eagle Inn.

He never cast suspicion on the goddesses of the Pantheon.

EYE-CATCHING

Elizabeth Hammerstein was stretching her body in front of her upstairs window in the Spread Eagle Inn. The exercise was clearing her head. She had been so strangely influenced by the shining heavenly body that was the moon. She was reeling from the magic of it.

She had succumbed to the Inspector's solid, male presence. Nothing more intriguing seemed at first to defy this very simple explanation. She found her thinking reduced to recalling his anglophile Burberry jacket and his lean, intelligent face peering out above the smart cut of what he was wearing. And he was clearly paying attention to what she said to him. It induced happiness, she thought, as so few of her male colleagues had ever thought her capable of womanly virtues—or for that matter, womanly feelings. She was captivated by Horatio's possessiveness. Indeed, she was pleased by it.

Now she struggled with the opposite, with consciously, not emotionally, clearing her head. At this moment all she wanted to know was what all his attention and her succumbing to it meant to her. She was left without the moon's subtle glow.

To be in love—what foolishness, she said to herself suddenly and decisively.

But, as she countenanced her emotions, she found herself not thinking of books and the explanations she was giving Inspector Queberon about Stourhead, but, instead, of this man who held her in thrall. He had awakened all her long neglected emotion.

The silvery sheen of the moon's lustrous light was beaming over her again, as it had done before. And it would do so again. She was caught, imprisoned, joyful.

She had gone to her bedroom later than expected. The Inspector and she had partaken of a substantial meal and talked animatedly about the style and invention of landscape gardens, eyes locked together. After so many trials, they wanted nothing but their own seclusion. They talked. They consciously avoided discussing criminality. What had brought them together was their own magic, arising ever more as their mutual interests. So they banished all else during their gazing into each other's eyes.

Elizabeth, to the amusement of Inspector Queberon, had vivaciously held forth that 'English' was applied to this type of garden all over the world, but Scotland had its fine share in the early days even.

"Take Inveraray on Loch Fyne for example, a stylish garden, and one of the first in the gothic architectural mode, good to look at, it was so romantic, and a portent of many things to come.

"And take the family of William Adam. His sons, John, Robert, and James and, most of all, he himself, made weighty contributions to the castle and to architecture. They were busy in the years it took to erect Inveraray, but also, and this was mainly Robert and James, finished monumental mansions and their ornaments in London."

She was looking vivaciously towards him, losing herself in his presence, even though overtly speaking about nothing other than what she knew.

Again Elizabeth had undivided attention; the Inspector was raptly aware. He would never use 'Scottish' and 'English' interchangeably again. He even forgot his meal. The physical was but a sideshow to his spiritual rapture.

. . .

Now it was the Inspector who was stretching in front of his window, alone in his room.

The landscape on his side caught the full lustre of the moon. Again they shared it, but his room was in the other side of the inn to Elizabeth's. The moon was high in the sky.

Identical thoughts and an identical outlook preoccupied his male mind. He was trying to make sense of this new swirling of emotions within him. He thought he might be able to introduce strict sanity. He was rapidly coming unstuck.

They were both looking out of windows at opposite but quite similar ends of the inn.

And only Elizabeth saw the ivy-clad man.

It was while she was stretching. She casually looked down from the window. Then she looked again and more closely, more intently. The figure was mighty strange, but it was definitely unlocking the car that belonged to James Owen.

Elizabeth did not have a car of her own. She spurned them in favour of bicycles. But now she needed to know where this particular vehicle was going.

Her immediate reaction was to alert the Inspector. She hoped very much he had another car available. However, she didn't know his room number. She raced to reception, throwing on her overcoat, all else that she was wearing being still intact; she had not yet undressed. When she ran down to the first floor, she practically shouted the Inspector's name, commanding the intimidated receptionist to call his room and make him come down to the hall. She was horribly excited and insistent. Then she ran out through the entryway.

The Inspector was relaxed and contemplating sweet dreams. When the phone rang, he was in no mood to answer it. It made him jump.

But answer he did and in a moment he, too, was electrified. He had the presence of mind to adjust his tie and shirt and pull on a knitted jumper on top of his trousers, but that was in passing.

Elizabeth ran down stairs and out the door to the near parking lot, and suddenly her gait modified on catching sight of Owen again; she ambled, as if nothing was concerning her; as if she had just inadvertently returned to retrieve something she had left outside. Out of the corner of her eye, she caught a macabre vision of ivy trailing green leaves and sprouts, clinging to the dark shape of the man she suspected beyond doubt to be James Owen. She sauntered closer.

As she was moving within range of him and as she was about to speak, he turned and lunged for her. He caught her wrist and arm and twisted them.

She gave a muffled cry. But he was fast and strong. He heaved her with one motion off the ground and into the boot of his car. He clamped it shut and immediately climbed into the driver's seat. The car was set in motion, the headlights turned on.

Just as he emerged, the Inspector saw two shapes. One shape he knew; a feminine form. He registered how she was thrown in the back, the boot had crashed down and shut tight. He heard a last gasp. All, it seemed, in a split second.

As the headlights showed which way the car was heading, Inspector Queberon ran to his own borrowed, holiday vehicle. Luckily he had made the choice of a powerful car. In true police fashion, he turned on the ignition, but not the lights. He followed the car that seemed to have ingested Elizabeth.

After following a road good for most cars, it turned off. The new road was dusty and rough. The seemingly unconcerned moon still hung high in the sky.

The Inspector was disconcerted. He was uncertain of the direction and still wary of driving on what for him was the wrong side of the road. The track seemed to roll uphill. The dirt clogged sideways and back. It was hard to see right in front, although the headlights of the car he was following were strongly visible.

Twists and turns and low-hanging briar bushes were no help. But in the distance, he made out the moonlit form of Alfred's Tower, its three brick sides now pale, but upstanding in the black and white light. The night gained brightness under the moon's arc.

Almost there, the kidnapper's car failed to make the grade upward; it stalled. The Inspector could hear swearing and the repeated grind of the starter tried and tried again. He saw a man, presumably James Owen, trailing ivy, jump from the driver's seat.

And then the man ran.

There was no telling if he had seen Queberon's car.

With the lights still off, the Inspector got out. He wasn't being slow, but he stumbled. Rather than chase Owen, he made a beeline for the trunk that enclosed Elizabeth. He jerked the driver's side open and released the trunk. He heard the snap of it opening. He heard tears and gasps, a woman giving vent to her feelings of being captured. A woman who thought her ordeal far from over.

Inspector Queberon gathered her in his arms. For a brief moment the two of them were one, united in soul and body. She even lowered her head on his shoulder and was wracked by sobs. He was more than awkward, patting her disarrayed hair.

Elizabeth swallowed all her emotions and her

fear of clammy, enclosed spaces. She squeezed Queberon's hand and absent-mindedly straightened his jacket. She said, "That's James Owen, the culprit. He's off to the top of the hill, to Alfred's Tower. Let's take the left-hand route and catch him before he has a chance to rearm. His gun is not on him, I should know."

They gingerly, by the light of the full moon, made their way around the left side of the Tower. They heard voices.

The light inside illuminated two heads. One was encased in wheat, the other in ivy; one of them was familiar to them. The two were talking animatedly.

Owen was urgently and wildly gesturing for Abdullah to round up all the guns. These looked really strange in their vegetative adornments.

Owen said, "Abdullah, I think Stourhead tainted. We should make it to Bristol. The car gave up on the last bend. I came to say, we're finished here. Let's abandon this quiet inland hidey-hole and go to sea."

Abdullah only grunted. She saw the need to hurry. She wasn't blind to Owen; she just wanted all the weapons to be gathered up; this cache she hoped would succeed in replenishing spent arms needed to support the revolution.

While they bent to their task of rounding up the

guns, not made easy by the slippery wheat and the obstinate ivy, the light shone on their bent backs. The figure of Hercules, with his lion's skin and cudgel, was a shadow in a corner. They had incurred the wrath of the gods more than usual. They had trespassed in the temples. They had violated sacred places.

Hercules, muscular, but scantily clad, raised his shadowy cudgel. The lion's skin, although hollow-eyed and nothing fleshly, had ambition to bite. This ménage of viciousness was righteous. Without much weight in physical terms, it closed in on the bent figures. It approached much as veterans would on a Herculean task. It would ravage much as a lion intended.

Hercules pounded the ivy and the wheat. What was beneath received the same blows. His cudgel was much in action. But all that could be seen was outlines and imprints. It was hard to tell anyone here was a god engaged in punishment of infidels. The empty lion skin had much fun in biting buttocks. It licked its lips and gave a lioness and lion's roar, alternating.

It didn't take long. The Herculean task was finished before it started, even; the two figures involved in using Stourhead to their own ends were sitting on the floor. They raised their arms above their heads to ward off further blows. Much worse, they were being tickled up their noses by the vegetation Ceres had produced. Their inane laughter went up to the rafters. Abdullah and Owen were doubled over in both senses of being beaten to the floor and laughing because they couldn't help it.

The Inspector and Elizabeth looked through the door, cracked open only a slit, in wonder. They were outclassed.

The rusted nails that kept the placard for Alfred high on the wall of the Tower suddenly snapped. It glided down in the moonlight and at their feet was outlined in black. The lettering said: *Liberty*.

Inspector Queberon sighed with relief. Elizabeth tried to peer more closely at the shadowy outline she was convinced had Herculean proportions. But nothing decisive could be seen.

THE MOON WENT BEHIND A CLOUD.

Both of them left things as they were. Neither one wished to interfere where greater powers had intervened.

The car was where the Inspector had abandoned it. Very quiet and dark, the hubcaps stood out in a silver sheen. The Mercedes purred. This was very strange, as the motor was shut down.

Owen and Abdullah moved creakily on all fours.

Their arms and legs were just enough to transport them. They took nothing but the clothes on their backs; nothing but the ever-sprouting vegetation Ceres had introduced. This contributed much to the amusement of Isis.

LOVE IS IN THE EYE OF THE BEHOLDER

The decision to leave revenge to the gods and goddesses was a good one, Elizabeth thought. She was pleased to see vegetative action taken. Better madness meted out to those having no thoughts on the death of others than to imprison them. The culprits had met with a just supernatural fate for their human avarice and Owen's blighted thoughts. He would babble and be incomprehensible. And his weaponry would be wheat. "Substance to be used to make good bread, if anyone is willing to harvest what is surely evil failure," she added. "The grey-clothed lady can simply flee—I'm convinced she has learned to invest her energy elsewhere."

Without touching a thing, she persuaded Horatio Queberon to quit Alfred's Tower.

They found Owen's abandoned car stuck in the dirt, a dreadful mud-spattered hulk and worthy of avoidance. They left it behind.

THE INSPECTOR CLIMBED into his rented vehicle and took the driver's seat. After a moment, Elizabeth opened the passenger door of his Mercedes and got in, too.

Each felt anticlimactic; a climb downwards spiritually and slowly from all they had seen. Queberon was reticent. But Elizabeth lent over.

She touched his cheek and said, "Leave the culprits to it. Revenge is being taken for the madness of their trespass."

The Inspector sat there. He was thinking his own thoughts. He turned to Elizabeth.

"It's a far country, Germany, but it has its merits. I don't know if you'd enjoy it. Come anyway. So much of it is practical, some of it is romantic. I want to show you. I know you've seen it, but not with me. We could celebrate with its best wines and admire its best views."

In her dazed state, still filled with admiring the acts of the gods and goddesses which profoundly touched her, Elizabeth was lacking in thought. It was this very blankness that made her receptive. She didn't even know she was a candidate for sweet and entertaining meals and pleasant adventures. All at once she liked being cosseted for what she was, not for what she knew. She liked the idea of not having to be anything other than herself.

Queberon went on, "We could tour east and west. Germany is still split in spirit. But you'd get the flavour of both. And you could further your skills and investigations."

Elizabeth was filled with the absurdity of the situation. Here they were, Queberon speculating on her knowledge and the new Germany and this while they were still sitting on a dirt road in an eighteenth-century landscape garden under the full moon. Its beams were luminous and reaching out to them. And in practical terms, no one even knew whether this, Queberon's hired car, would start again on this muddy road.

She said, starting to hiccup, "Yes, I'll go wherever you'll go." She was absurdly happy suddenly and became madly generous at this very moment, as mad as the full moon.

Queberon looked at her. Kissed her ardently. Then he attempted to start the car. It wouldn't go, either forward or backward; they were stuck.

Nothing for it, but to get out and walk, hoping in the lustrous, moonlit dark to find their way. They held hands as they went.

· · ·

ABDULLAH AND OWEN struggled with the heavily overgrown weapons. They returned to their own car, got it started, pulled it close to the Tower as the moon was setting and casting the longest shadows. They stashed all they could in the back seat and opened the trunk. Then they were going to fill the car and hand each other more goods. It was to be an efficient manoeuvre and they would get away. They would then bathe and drown the wheat and the ivy.

They filled the back seat. Now, they each thought, for the trunk. The roomy trunk was open.

In its depths was a new blackness. Something stirred. Owen started. Here was not a human carcass, but a roaring beast. He seemed to see a wild boar. But how could he see a wild boar in his utterly sanitised and orderly, mechanical vehicle? He looked again at this shadowy, rutting beast that he was now seeing.

Owen, in a quavering voice, said to his friend Abdullah, "Look into this trunk, will you, and tell me what you see."

Abdullah thought her friend not a little strange, but nonetheless decided to humour him. "Nothing," she said.

"Nothing," repeated Owen testily. "Nothing. But don't worry about this nothing as you'll be impaled just as I will be by raving tusks as soon as you pile in the goods." He added this in a wavering undertone, a scared one.

Nothing was apparent. Abdullah saw nothing.

Owen felt he was truly going insane.

He made Abdullah stack the guns.

The guns, unfortunately, were full of wheat that grew wildly on all and everything. But Owen insisted, seeing to it that it was well tied up, roping all of it into the trunk. Abdullah was hampered, too, with the magnitude of the fast sprouting wheat.

Owen was sick and wretched on the side of the road. His head was lowered into his hands. Then he glanced up. He had a bitter taste in his mouth. But he saw clearly enough. And it was a fine statue of lyrical proportions: a beautiful young man, gleaming all in white. He had a waving cape, held over his hand. Owen recalled that a statue very like him was in the Pantheon. What's more, this figure was an active protagonist for republican values, fighting a rampaging wild boar to save his people from death.

Meleager now was half-hidden by beech trees. And half revealed by the full moon.

He seemed to approach rapidly in the direction of the car. Meleager had his hunting dog with him. The greyhound was sniffing the air. It was nearing the muddy dirt road on which the car was pulled up the bank. The hunting dog was leaping through the trees as if they were not there.

Meleager floated. He was facing Owen and that was what Owen fervently wished he could avoid. Meleager came directly towards him.

Owen buried his face in the cold grass. He was bending over to hide. Abdulla tried to straighten him, tried to make him walk. The ivy was growing out his nose and up into his hair, hair that had been so neat up to now. Owen screwed his eyes shut. He shook off Abdullah.

There was nothing for it, but for Abdullah to drag Owen to the car. She would have to drive. She hoped the car would start. At last, it leapt off the mound of grass and sand. She barely managed to control it.

In the plunge forward, Owen opened his eyes. In his fixed stare the wild boar was close. Meleager, all white and beautiful, came ever nearer. So did his hunting dog. The two seemed to converge on Owen.

The boar leapt then, too, and seemed to toss Owen sideways. One of the tusks went clean through him. All at once, Meleager swiftly ran towards the wild boar. Upheaval ensued, but the man-god skewered the boar. Owen was caught in the middle, but they seemed not to see him.

Owen seemed lacking in human substance, but he was everywhere in the way. Wherever he ducked, wherever he lay not moving, the wild boar and Meleager fought the same battle, again and again. He seemed to attract them, and yet they seemed to disregard him.

He was more than tired and worn out. He was ready to flee.

The last man normally stationed in the Pantheon was, though disregarding Owen in every way, centring on him and repeating that Owen was trapped in his every fight against the wild boar.

Meleager was getting the better of him. And here Owen had thought he was as tough as nails, ready to meet any competition weighing in against him.

James Owen had liked being in the right, and in the money; in fact he disdained others for their want of lucrative aims. But now he gave in, he shivered and declared himself defeated by moonlit ghosts. He had trespassed on the sanctity of the gods and they were having none of it. Owen had lost.

Abdulla saw Owen cower and become prostrate and get up and lie flat on his back again. She saw nothing, but the strange behaviour of her friend, who spoke gibberish until deathly silence descended.

She packed her friend into the car a second time. It was in the nick of time, too. Owen's eyes started rolling, each in a different direction. Wheat and ivy were growing all over the car. Time to get out, Abdullah thought. Time to leave this infernal ground.

She spun the car onto the dirt track. She took it in the direction of Bath. She followed the dirt track to the road, and did not look back. Never would she visit Stourhead again, nor think with kindness on Alfred's Tower.

The moon shone bright and the valley Abdullah left behind her gleamed with renewed beauty; it was itself again.

Abdullah drove on, but she had to admit that all was in vain. Even her grey wool outfit had succumbed and been supplanted by wild wheat.

She would drive to Bath, but never finish the plan they had concocted. Every weapon was out of action.

STOURHEAD REVISITED

The Inspector went early to alert the National Trust, using all his official qualifications. He alerted them to the salient facts. The culprits had to face earthly justice, but that was out of his hands. He was, after all, still on holiday and suspected privately that James Owen would not regain sanity.

He wound his way down again from the heights to the valley below and the Spread Eagle Inn. It was a glorious morning and the sun was rising in the sky. In the distance he could see the bright disc on top of Henry Hoare's Obelisk. It was beckoning. A little to the left, between the red rhododendrons, the pleasant warm stone of Apollo's Temple was gleaming. The Inspector was happy to have done his duty and was at peace with the world.

As he re-entered the inn, he glimpsed Elizabeth, somewhat tousled, seated at a table. She had been, no doubt, looking for him, wanting to coordinate their witness statements and wondering what to say about capturing Abdullah and James Owen. This was not an easy task since their fate had been sealed by gods and goddesses. Who would believe her or him?

Bowing to gods and goddesses would be proper, but who would say to her she was right? And yet both she and he, an inspector of police, had witnessed the action—and its consequences. They both looked outwardly respectable—but would they be believed?

She looked up. There in his sombre Burberry jacket and brown corduroy trousers, wearing his habitual white shirt, only unbuttoned slightly for his holiday, was Horatio Queberon. She smiled.

Hailing him, she said, "I was convinced you'd gone to the gateway that contains the offices of the National Trust, their modern office up the hill. I wanted us to speak with one voice, so I waited to talk to you. But you went there ahead of me. I'll forgive you this once." Again she smiled.

He came over to her. He looked benignly down on her. He wasn't going to argue. He said, "I did everything as you would have wanted. *Alles.* I told them who they were looking for, and that they seemed headed for Bath. Their car was spattered with mud and had wheat, most unseasonal, growing within. They were good about it, despite this last fact, which no one seemed to believe, but they credited what I had to say.

"Let us have the peace of the moment, now the sun is shining. Let's finish breakfast and go out into this glorious valley, where from the Palladian Bridge the sightline is up to the Pantheon. We have much to be grateful for, although we'll never really know the whole truth of the matter."

The Inspector continued, "You have been kind to share so much of your knowledge. I'd just like to amble on now, without anything turbulent intervening, and digest what you've said. I'll have this factual and interpretive reverie. You could join me and we could walk the length and breadth of Stourhead again. We could just enjoy."

Horatio Queberon gestured towards the sun that was ever climbing to its heights. He knew this was a special trait on such a fine day. He also knew Apollo, the sun god, was kindly inclined to favour such investigative frivolity. Horatio liked the temple with all its festive columns and big lion-bite sized, circling entablature. It was worthy of Apollo to have the only temple in the valley with such a grand view over all of it. It looked over the whole encompassing, dancing joyousness of Stourhead.

He was eager to be out on a day like this. But he was ever mindful of Elizabeth.

So Inspector Queberon pulled out a chair, but squirmed in restless fashion on it, waiting impatiently for Elizabeth to finish and go with him. She didn't draw breakfast out; she was considerate and gulped it down and stood up, joining him, taking her light coat off the back of her chair.

They went out into the fine morning. It was a special festive weekend with music in the wonderful green places that Stourhead held out. They saw immediately that choirs had positioned themselves in many places along the lake and on the heights. The joyful choirs coincided with how both of them felt. And their souls joined in the soaring music wafting into the bright sunshine.

As they sauntered, the yellow azaleas twinkled among the trees and on their walk. The flowering bushes added the scent of lemons and clear virtue. The lake gave of its blue happiness and it reflected the sky.

They joined hands again and looked with appreciation up at the Pantheon. They were on the side of the lake which gave such a splendid view. The simple but effective stone of soft coloured beige of which the Pantheon was made protruded from the hanging spring-green wood behind and around it. The dome hid the opeion, the eye to heaven. In it the gods would languish until they were once more roused.

Hercules was perhaps the most prominent. He had his cudgel by his wrestler's body. The skin of the lion was draped to effect. He was proud.

To complement this half-god, the human, but strong, Meleager was on a pedestal. He, too, had fought on behalf of his people against a vicious wild boar which was laying the countryside and towns to waste. He had triumphed and was celebrated for his good deed ever since. He was an example of the value of serving the public.

In the niches, but stepping out, were the goddesses, augmenting the men, and in this case, happy to do so. The first goddess was Isis, the Great Mother. Her tribute was meant for all the many people who came after her. She had migrated from the East and yet maintained her powers.

Then there was Diana, known to many as the goddess Artemis, her Greek name, and a fierce virgin. She hunted in the woods with her retinue. Diana was the patroness of the mysterious woods, but she was also the moon goddess. Whenever the moon was duplicated in the fathomless waters of a lake, a stream, or the sea, she came into her own.

The painter Turner, indebted to Henry Hoare's nephew Sir Richard Colt-Hoare, sketched Lake Nemi where Diana appeared as the moon, floating on the edge of the Otherworld, the waters a gateway in the round crater that once was a volcano.

She was augmented by Ceres, the goddess that brings plenty in the summers of fruitfulness. Ceres had lost Persephone, her daughter, and spring is now and evermore the time of their meeting. At Ceres' command all the fruits of the earth, especially wheat, which sustains the human race, rises and matures on earth. She is all-powerful, because without her, the world would starve.

Susanna, the last woman of the goddesses, is more Christian. Although not needed this time, she was a favourite of Henry Hoare's because her name chimed with that of his wife and daughter.

These goddesses and mighty half-gods served in Henry Hoare's Pantheon. He gave them space and the worship due in secular gardens, but as one who knows their powers well.

Elizabeth and the Inspector vividly joined in this festival honouring the power of Stourhead. They were now around the lake again and descending to the grotto.

It was dark, but the sun was shining on the lake into which the Stour poured its waters.

The nymph was languid, watching how the waters spilled out. She was reclining, but careful to note who was passing. It was cool in her shade, and the pool assembled below her.

They saw the ever-renewing English village. It was waiting for the leaves to reach their freshest spring green. The church of St. Peter and the medieval Bristol Cross combined together over the five arches of the bridge. This was a pretty picture and permanent, in each season.

The Inspector and Elizabeth walked in this cool, underground habitat of the grotto until they reached its true guardian, the River God. His brilliant white head and his long hair faced them. His hand was pointing upwards, forever pointing to the path to be taken. It was the one of virtue, upwards to the Pantheon. This was as yet hidden from the view of those looking outward to the lake from the grotto. But whether hidden from view or obvious, it honoured consequence, from the activities of Hercules, who had achieved so much, to Isis, the Great Mother, who reigned over earth's happenings.

All revelled in this morning's idyll, the essence of Stourhead, its gushing waters, the foundation and the spilling out of the river towards the sunny day. The pottery bowl lying at the River God's side contained the waters of life.

A NOTE FROM AUTHOR JOANNA PATERSON

After an academic career, creative fiction began late in life, but reflects my urge to lift knowledge gained about past events and people to imaginative heights. Themes can be elaborated, given crucial extensions, even humorous episodes, while still retaining real landscapes and places.

Writing helped to surmount my disability after my stroke that happened soon after my retirement. And all my writing is meant to challenge, but also to bring enjoyment.

If you've enjoyed reading this book, please look out for the rest of the series to see what else is in store for Elizabeth Hammerstein and Inspector Queberon. Please also spread the word with a review on Amazon, Goodreads, Waterstones, Kobo or any other suitable forum. These are immensely helpful.

You can keep up to date with my writing, and see some of my artwork inspired by the landscape gardens that feature in my novels at sibylpress.com.

ACKNOWLEDGMENTS

A huge Thank You to Jim Paterson, my husband, for both the mundane tasks that are so challenging in everyday work when caring for the disabled and the intellectual talent he has that helped me a great deal when publishing this book. And importantly I owe much gratitude to Claire Wingfield for her undaunted courage in paying attention to every detail in reading this book from start to finish. She also helped edit this book and did more than anyone in accepting both the humour and the seriousness of characters and setting.

Lightning Source UK Ltd.
Milton Keynes UK
UKHW040659071120
372984UK00002B/181